Death in l'Acadie

a Kesk8a story

www.crowecreations.ca

Death in l'Acadie: a Kesk8a story

First Crowe Creations Publication March 2015

This is a work of fiction set against a backdrop of history.

Front cover photo © iStock: 09-22-08 © wynnter
(Patron Saint of Canada, Jean de Brebeuf (1593–1649) is illustrated confronting a Huron Indian council in his efforts to convert the nation to Christianity. Brebeuf enjoyed some success before being brutally tortured and martyred in 1649. Engraved by an unknown artist, it was published in 1879 and edited by John O'Kane Murray and is now in the public domain.)

Cover Design © 2015 Crowe Creations
Interior design by Crowe Creations
Text set in Garamond; headings in Clarity Gothic SF

Crowe Creations
ISBN:978-1-927058-27-5

CreateSpace
ISBN-13: 978-1511501156
ISBN-10: 1511501154

For my daughter, Patricia, and my brother, Bill,
both possessing and possessed by Acadian DNA.
How many of us are there?

Acknowledgements

Abundant thanks go to:

Phyllis Bohonis
Lyse Coté
Evelyn Crete
Albert Dumont
Warren Guidry
Grandfather Joe
Suzanne Keeptwo
Bill McKay
Sue Pictou
Joanne Samson
Christopher Snowboy
Marcel St-Amand
The Native Learning Circle (Ottawa)
Joe Wilmot

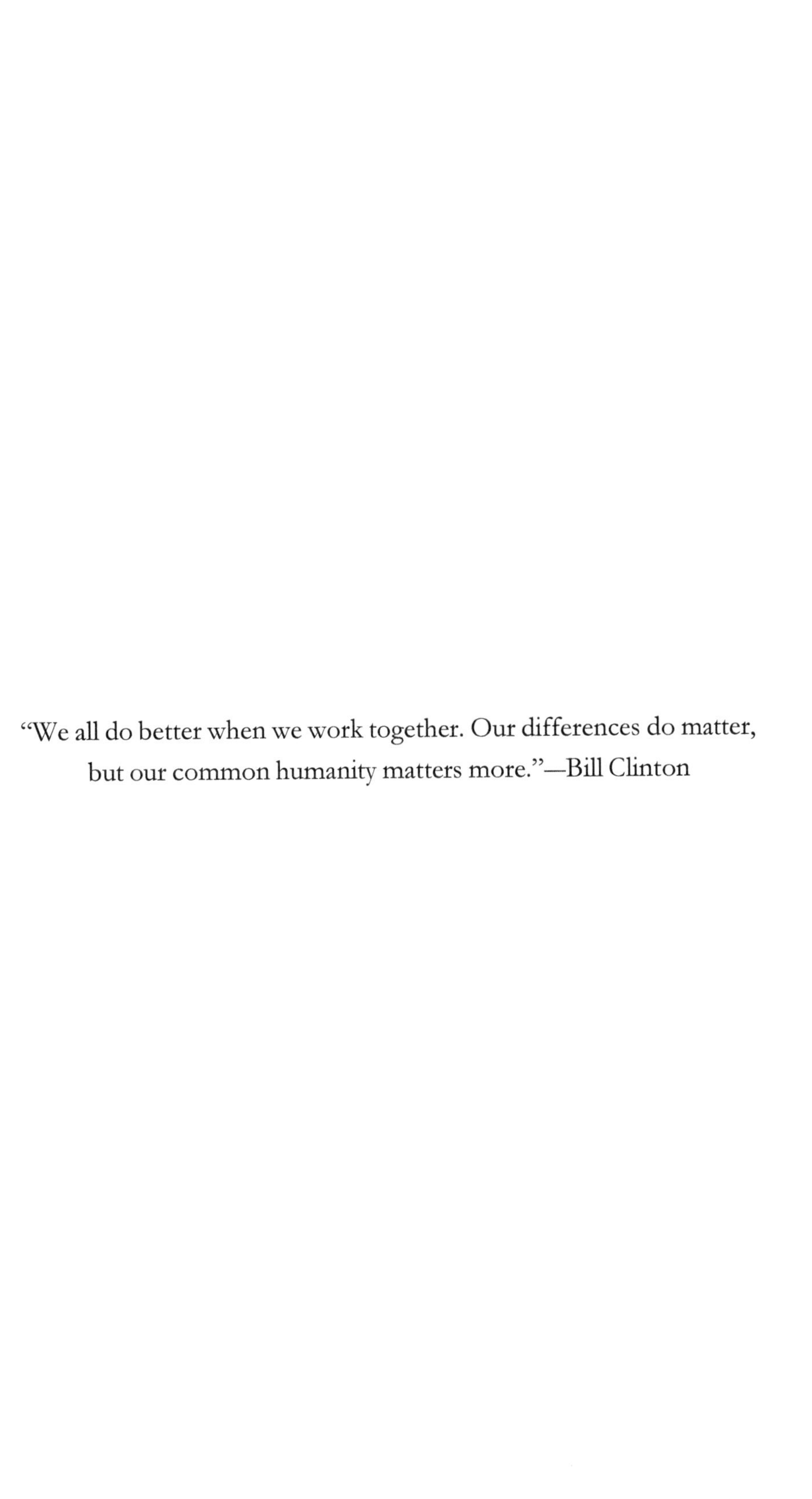

"We all do better when we work together. Our differences do matter, but our common humanity matters more."—Bill Clinton

c. 1678–81 Port Royal, Acadia (Present-day Annapolis Royal NS)

One

When I told my friend Feather that I wanted to lay with the Father, she was horrified and told me I had to go to Confession right away or I'd go to Hell for sure. "And I told you," she added. "Don't call me Feather no more. Call me Hélène."

"Feathery Hélène. Hélène-y Feather." I loved to get her going so I could watch her eyes flashing at me like I was Father Soucy's Devil that he was always talking about.

"You wouldn't know what to do anyways," she said. "You never laid with a man." She was talking to me like she was many, many winters older than I was but she was only two winters older.

"I see… And you did. You know all about it."

Her face went all red. "Of course not."

"Of course not? Feather—whose name should really be Oh Look That Soldier Is So Handsome—is telling me that she didn't lay with that special man of hers yet?" I was getting to her good. I had to walk faster to keep up with her now. "Isn't telling an untruth one of those things the Father is always talking about? What does he call them? Ah, *les péchés*. Sins."

"Of course it is. And it's a bigger sin to lay with a man. And stop calling me Feather."

"We are getting impatient to become women, alors, nous devons nous dépêcher à commettre des péchés. E'e? Yes?"

"Stop with your poésie absurde. That doesn't even make sense. 'We must hurry to commit sins.' What kind of nonsense is that? You'll never be any good as a storyteller if you go around making up things like that all the time."

"I was making a joke," I said. "Dépêcher … des péchés…?"

She didn't react other than to walk even faster.

"Never mind." Feather had become much too serious since she and her handsome soldier from the fort had become close friends and she had started listening to the Father about how she should be acting around the rest of us now that she was a young woman of fifteen winters. "You seem to be in quite a hurry… *Hélène*."

"I'm walking fast because I'm trying to get away from you. *Marie-Thérèse*."

Sometimes she could make me laugh really hard. This was one of the times I had to grab my stomach and lean over. "That's not what I meant and you know it… *Feather*." She disappeared around a corner in the path. When I stopped laughing, I had to run to catch up to her.

It felt funny having to call her Hélène all the time when she had a perfectly good Mi'gmaw name. Same with me. I hated the name Marie-Thérèse. Well, to tell you the truth, I hated my real name, Keskoua, too. It had been chosen for me by one of the Grandfathers two winters before but if I pronounced the second part of it as Segewa't, then it sounded better. It then meant what Sun did every day and Moon did every night:

they rose. That made my name beautiful and bright. When the Fathers wrote my name on their papers, they wrote it with a number in it—"Kesk8a"—so when somebody read it, they would know enough to say the "ou" part through their nose. We already knew how to pronounce it so we didn't need to write it down with a strange symbol. We didn't write very much down and when we did, we sometimes used birch bark or hides but we didn't bring all the writings with us every time we went to another camp. We would carry a map until we knew how to get there from our memory. We had enough wikuom birch bark and other things to carry on our backs. Even the little ones carried things to help out. We had to carry our stories in our heads. That was the responsibility Kji Niskam—the Great Spirit—was training me for.

I didn't really want to lay with Father Soucy. Not at all. He was stiff and proper—and I knew a Father would never, ever lay with a woman—so it was great fun to make him uncomfortable. He was young for a Father. You never got to know anything personal like their age or anything like that about them, but you could tell for a Father he was a young one, under thirty winters old.

He was tall and thin with light brown hair and eyes and he always looked somewhere between mad and sad; and over his trousers he always wore a long black dress—with purple trim—which would make me mad and sad too if I had been a man. I mean, wearing black was bad enough but wearing women's clothing must have been hard for him to do in front of people. His church was made entirely of wood and except for the painted wooden saints inside that he had sent somebody all the way to the settlement at Québec to get, and the colored-glass windows that came overland off a ship, he pretty well built it by himself. If you measured between Port Royal (where Feather's soldier lived) and our village, the Father's church was about half way between but closer to our village. He was overheard to say many times that the soldiers and everyone else who lived at the fort were already baptized and trained to obey God's will, so he needed now to concentrate on teaching "les sauvages" how to behave like civilized, decent people. "La conquête des âmes est la tâche la plus importante de notre temps. The conquest of souls is the most vital endeavor of our times." He always whispered "the conquest of souls" part but he didn't need to, our people had become very familiar with those words since the first Newcomers in their black dresses had arrived in our land. Father Soucy built his wooden house beside his church but by then some of our people were talking to him and listening to what he had to say and going to Mass so they helped him with that.

When I sat in Mass in the front row of log seats which I liked to be in because I knew it made him nervous (and it got my Feathery friend Hélène going, too), I would lift my dress up to just below my knees so he could see my long beautiful shins between my hem and the top of my boots. She would scold me after Mass for petting my knees when the little bell rang while he was trying to change the bread into God's body and the moqopa'q, the wine, into God's blood. It was supposed to be the "holiest" time during Mass (she reminded me each time I did it), and he was supposed to act "holy." He usually did, but he sometimes looked at the people (me) over top of those strange eye glasses of his with their ribbons looped over his ears—and which made his eyes look like they belonged on somebody else's face. I was glad he used them only during the Mass to read from his special book.

"You will go to Hell, Marie-Thérèse. You will, you will! Aren't you afraid of the Devil one little bit?" Feather asked me this after Mass one day as we walked to our village together.

"Not one bit. I am more afraid of Claude Guidry's pig than I am of Father Soucy's Devil."

"I will pray for you," said my friend with her face all serious and sad like the Father's always was. "As hard as I can. And what do you know of

Claude Guidry's pig?" Before I could say anything about this, she stopped walking and turned to face me, looking up at me because I was tall and she was short like her mother was. "Claude Guidry is over thirty summers old. How do you know him?" Her eyes narrowed and her lips wrinkled inward. "Does he even have a pig?"

"He has a pig. A big mean reddish-brown one that he took off a floundered slaver at Wreck Cove two summers ago. A couple of times a year, Claude takes his pig to one of the boars in the fort for her to have baby pigs, and when she has her babies she is more dangerous than a moose at the rut."

I knew of the mean old sow ever since the time I had walked past the back of Claude Guidry's house when he was outside in his main corral, way back under the roof of one of the open sheds. His house was north of our village and he had built it before the last full moon in only one day with the help of everybody in our community, several coureurs de bois (the runners of the woods) and even some men from the fort. I was on my way to check on some sweetgrass my mother had set out to dry up past there.

He was hollering to someone, anyone, to shut the gate while he wrestled with a huge red pig. Seven or eight young red piglets ran loose inside a smaller paddock, squealing like their little hearts were breaking. Because his house was some distance away from our village, it appeared that nobody else but me could hear him struggling with his pig.

There was such a commotion going on and Claude Guidry seemed to be so angry that I was afraid to do anything at first. I figured out quickly that he had wanted to separate the piglets from the sow and things had got out of hand. It wasn't only the compound's outer back gate that needed closing—I could see from where I was that one of the slats was cracked and sticking out like something had fallen against it, and the gate was slowly swinging open, widening the gap, and I could tell that the pig was watching it, too—but the gate between the piglets and the sow also needed closing.

"What do you want me to do?" I yelled, trying not to laugh as he rolled around in the pig shit with the big red sow half on top of him, then half under him. "Do you want me to climb the fence here? Or go around to the back?"

The words coming out of his mouth would have made Feather cross herself a hundred times. "Shut the back gate, hostie, you stupid girl!"

"That's not very nice to say to me, Monsieur Claude Guidry. Ask me nice."

"Hostie, tabernacle! This pig will crush me to death before you listen to what I am saying! Shut the back gate! For the love of God, shut the back gate. Please!"

I was going to do it anyway because it looked like he was in a dangerous situation. When he said please, it made me move quicker. So I went around and stepped inside the main compound securing the damaged back gate behind me. Then I circled round the inside of the corral's fence toward him and his red pig so the frightened little pigs would run away from me to the far side of their own paddock and not toward their mother and Claude Guidry. I walked past him and his pig and I fastened his other gate for him.

"Merci, damoiselle. I thought I was going to lose all of them. And the little ones are all sold for the end of summer after I fatten them up."

"That pig has a wickedly evil mind of her own by the look of her eyes," I said. And I meant it, too. "She looks mean. You should call her Orignal-Sale because she is like a dirty, mean moose. And she has stiff brown hairs like a moose, too." The thoughts of what her skin must feel like made my nose twitch.

His laughter made me feel like I was somebody important for a change and not just some young girl coming up to thirteen winters that everybody told to "go away and don't bother me" all the time.

"She's like that only when she has young," he said. "A word of advice to you. I wouldn't let the Grandfathers hear you saying such things about moose. Are they not a sacred animal?"

"They are. But I don't like them after what one of them did to Apalqaqamej."

"Who?"

"Chipmunk."

"I see."

"The big mean thing hurt her. And she was just trying to caress its baby."

"I'd forgotten about that," he said. "But I still wouldn't let them hear you talking like that. It's disrespectful. And it doesn't make you look good, either."

"Are you going to tell on me?"

"You saved my life today. I won't betray you. What do they call you?"

I had a feeling Claude Guidry already knew my name but I told him anyway. "Keskoua. It means Sunrise but I'm going to change it to Breaking of the Dawn."

"I don't think so." I liked his smile an awful lot. "It means you're a pain in the arse, doesn't it?"

"It does not!"

"And you aren't allowed to change it." He clucked at his pig and gently nudged her prickly reddish-brown side with his knee until she grunted and condescended to waddling around the shed into the enclosure behind it where the barn stood beneath a snawe'l, a sugar tree. He latched the gate. "Your mother is Martinique is she not?" He wiped his hands on the sides of his white flannel shirt. His dark blue pants were full of dust and mud and pig shit, and he leaned back against the fence to look me up and down. I could see that his eyes were not brown after all, but green.

"Your eyes are green," I said. "I've never seen such a thing!"

"Are they?" He seemed surprised. "And how many of them do I have, exactly?"

I knew some of the other Frenchmen from around, but Claude Guidry was completely different. He'd showed up not off a ship but from out of the forest, exhausted, filthy, smelling of fear and dressed like a Newcomer about nine summers earlier. I don't have to tell you he caused quite a stir among our people for arriving like that. They named him La Verdure, the Woodsman, just because he'd survived the bush without knowing how. After that, he spent so much time learning the bush he always seemed a stranger and ended up becoming one of the coureurs de bois all the women who had the bad luck to get involved with one said you should never get involved with. The Runners of the Woods were never home and you got awful lonely when your husband was away all the time when you were still young and you got pregnant every time he came home, and sometimes you lost the babies, and sometimes you died doing it and it was always alone. The money was good, so you had everything you needed. Except your man. In the days before the White people came and built the forts where our people had to go to trade, the men, women and children would travel together which was the way of our people. But after the White people came, things changed and we got greedy for their guns, their metal knives, and their many tools and trinkets that made our lives easier. We taught some of them how to trap and hunt and survive in the bush. They learned on their own how to take our women. There were some said every coureur de bois had one of our women at each end of his trail and some in between, but a lot of that was just talk by the bitter old women whose husbands had left one day and had never come back. I would have said that a man like Claude Guidry would have had a woman at both ends of his trail and also at the end of each day's journey along the way. To have him talking to me like this and laughing at everything I said was something I never would have even dreamed of let alone thought.

"You have the same number of eyes as anyone else I've ever met except for One-Eyed Joe who has none anymore. Well he has one missing and the other one might as well be. He can barely see out of it. You have two. What a stupid question to ask!"

"So damoiselle is calling me stupid now." He smiled again. "Come help me feed my little piglets before they realize their maman is gone away."

So until he went back to the bush that winter to tend to his traplines, I helped him feed his reddish-brown piglets and we started becoming friends because I would drop in every few days to visit with him and Orignal-Sale. I would pet one or two of his growing piglets while he told me about his life before he came to l'Acadie and life among the Mi'gmaq.

The following summer I didn't visit with him until shortly before he left for the bush because I got my first Moon Time. This meant there were many ceremonies to honor this special time in my life. The whole community was happy for me. It was an important event and I was proud that I had become a woman. But at the same time I hated it: partly because it let everybody in the whole village know it would soon be time for me to take a husband even though I didn't want one; partly because the young boys teased me all the time now even though their mothers scolded them for doing it; and mostly because I didn't want Claude Guidry to know that I was different now even though I hoped he would notice that I wasn't a child anymore.

But the summer after that, the one when I was coming up to my fifteenth winter, I spent a lot of time with him even though One-Eyed Joe's woman had told me to be careful around men now that my breasts were large and my hips had widened. She told me she had a dream that something bad was going to happen to me unless I believed her and heeded her warning. Of course I didn't believe her. She was crazy. However, because

I hated to see that sadness behind her eyes whenever she reminded me of her dream, I told her I believed her, which I did in a way. I believed her enough to stop flirting with the Father at least, knowing full well she meant I had to watch myself around Claude Guidry, the Frenchman.

As it turned out we were both wrong. After all, I was young and she was crazy.

But she was also right. She was crazy for a reason. The same reason One-Eyed Joe had only one eye.

Two

Some people called One-Eyed Joe's woman Elue'wiet because she was crazy, but she had good reason to be crazy, I guess. Everybody had hated her mother when she was alive because she was very arrogant. Emtesgit, Snooty, was what a lot of the people called her mother behind her back; others called her mother Gesmi'sit because of her terrible accent. The accent wasn't her fault, of course. Her mother was nearly thirty winters old when Pierre Le Blanc dragged her skinny rear end into our village and then just left her there on her own while he went back to running the woods. He never returned. When our people got to know what her mother was like, some of them would laugh and say that Pierre left her behind because he was smarter than most of us thought he was. Her mother was Haudenosaunee, what the French called "les Iroquois," so none of the Newcomers trusted her at all and this made us wonder about her, too. Although we didn't have anything to do with the Haudenosaunee, we heard tales from the Newcomers about what they did to people if they captured them. None of it sounded right to me but it still made you wonder.

She was pregnant with One-Eyed Joe`s woman when Pierre left her behind in the village or else our people would have liked to let her starve to death on her own even though this was not our way. But she was good to help our women with many of their tasks and she had brought with her a special skill for making and decorating clothing. Her leather quillwork was better than any of the women in our village could do and she would teach anybody who asked her how to do it. But it all went to her head and she acted as though our women were inferior. I didn't know it then, but I heard stories later that her own mother had been taken from the Wendat, the Huron, by a Haudenosaunee man and it was her Wendat mother who had taught her to do flowers with quills. Living with the Haudenosaunee was how the mother of One-Eyed Joe's woman learned—from her own mother—that being an outsider can make you feel low if you don't accept them the same way they were willing to accept you.

When she had Pierre Le Blanc's baby—who grew up to be One-Eyed Joe's woman—she refused to let the priest at the fort baptize it, saying all priests were possessed with evil spirits. She would burn sweetgrass and pray for hours any time after he had come close to her or had spoken to her. When the child was about nine summers old, she went down to the edge of the ocean and walked all the way in, drowning herself. The mother of One-Eyed Joe took in the child and called her Young Rabbit Woman until the bad thing that made her crazy—and cost Joe one of his eyes—happened and then the people called her Elue'wiet, Crazy. But I still called her Young Rabbit Woman because the name Elue'wiet just reminded her of the bad thing and made her sad. I didn't like to make anyone sad.

By the time Young Rabbit Woman had passed her seventeenth summer, she was a beautiful young woman. I think a lot of our men thought she was beautiful just because she was foreign—half French, and the other half Haudenosaunee and Wendat—and she had light brown eyes instead of dark like ours, but she was beautiful in her own right. She was lithe and strong in body and able to outrun the women and some of the men when we held our races. Our Lnu Saqamaw, our Chief, had his eye on her for marriage to his second son thinking she would produce physically and morally strong, intelligent children. And he also thought if his son loved her enough he might stop drinking moqopa'q—wine—and beer and getting into fights with our people and with the French.

Unlike her mother, Young Rabbit Woman trusted and admired the Father and she went to Mass every day and made his meals, learning his foreign ways of cooking, although she said she never ate any of it. Everybody thought Young Rabbit Woman wasn't working as hard for the Father as she said she was. But she told me the Father wanted a lot of strange spices on his food that smelled awful and tasted worse so she couldn't eat it. That was why she always went back to her wikuom to eat after she prepared his meals. It wasn't anything else.

It wasn't only our own men who thought she was beautiful, some of the coureurs de bois who passed through our village tried to get her to travel along with them to be their woman. She would ignore these men and never spoke to any of them because she remembered everything her mother had told her about being taken from her people and abandoned among strangers.

It might have been better for Young Rabbit Woman to have run away into the bush to live by herself for the next few summers instead of not looking at or talking to Jean-Baptiste Bourque even when he followed her and stopped her on a trail whenever she was trying to get away from him. Her silence excited him. But it probably wouldn't have mattered anyway. Jean-Baptiste Bourque was typical of many of the coureurs de bois: he spent a lot of his time drinking and trying to get our people drunk so he could get away with cheating when he traded with them, even trading for their women sometimes. There were stories around that Jean-Baptiste took women with him all the time, even from faraway villages, and that nobody ever saw them again. They also said he had to take these women by force because nobody wanted to go with him willingly he was such a vicious drunk. And they said that once he clapped eyes on you, you belonged to him, whether you wanted to or not. So if you were even a little bit pretty, you were best to always stay in your wikuom and not even go out to relieve yourself when he was around.

So he clapped eyes on Young Rabbit Woman and it was only through the intervention of the Lnu Saqamaw and the Father that he didn't take her with him right away. He stayed around for days camped close to the village making everyone nervous because we knew there were some types of men you didn't dare push to anger. Then unexpectedly one morning he was no longer around when the people started waking up and going about the business of relieving themselves, washing themselves and preparing the morning's food. The people also noticed that the second son of the Lnu Saqamaw was walking all around the village waving a bottle half full of brandy and bragging that he was about to become the richest maudit Indian in l'Acadie.

He had "sold" his rights to Young Rabbit Woman, he claimed, to Jean-Baptiste Bourque on the promise of a big sum of money and all Second Son had to do was get her out to the coureurs de bois camp at Mouse Ridge. As usual, nobody believed him. One-Eyed Joe and Young Rabbit Woman hadn't heard him because they were on their way back from an overnight fishing trip half a day's journey away.

The Lnu Saqamaw wasn't Chief for nothing. He had come from a long line of wise men of good character but he and his ancestors had passed on to his second son only some of the former quality and not much of the latter one, so Second Son was smart enough to know that Young Rabbit Woman was not about to go any great distance into the bush alone with him, but would follow her foster brother, Joe, anywhere. Drunk as Second Son was, he was still able to convince Joe to come with him onto the land to look at something Second Son said was probably worth a lot of money. He led Joe to thinking it was gold he'd found.

"And we should bring Young Rabbit Woman with us. I think she'd like to see it, too," he said to Joe, Young Rabbit Woman standing right beside Joe, always eager, like I said, to follow him anywhere. So the three of them went into the bush and unknown to Joe (although he knew the way well, and should have realized where they were going), they headed to the coureurs de bois camp at Mouse Ridge where Jean-Baptiste Bourque and three of his fellow Runners waited for Young Rabbit Woman.

I think Joe caught on the moment they stepped into the clearing at Mouse Ridge camp and he saw Jean-Baptiste sitting there near the fire circle and grinning like a bobcat who had just sniffed at a pile of fox shit. But he wasn't expecting one of Jean-Baptiste's booty fellows to step up behind him and stick a knife under his chin.

"Allons-y," said the booty fellow. "Let's go." And he knocked Joe's musket out of his hand onto the ground and pushed him toward the kaksk'ug, the cedars, at the lower end of the camp. One of the other men picked up Joe's musket and leaned it against a side wall of the cabin that nestled under the snawe'g, the sugar trees, at the side of the clearing.

Second Son had snaked his arm around Young Rabbit Woman's throat from behind and was applying pressure against the side of her neck. Although she struggled like mad, kicking and trying to bite him, and was nearly as strong as he was, he managed to hold on until she slumped to the ground.

"I'll be glad to rid myself of this one," he said. "I don't know why you want her so bad, she's nothing but a priest-loving witch spirit. I'll never know what my father sees in her either. She'll never let you bed her, you know. I've tried and she's just too much trouble to be worth it."

"Mais, we'll see about that," said Jean-Baptiste Bourque, rising from the rock he was sitting on.

He started to unbutton his pants and as he did, the wide-eyed man who had picked up Joe's gun to lean it against the cabin wall murmured something and started to fidget, not with his buttons, but with something hanging from his belt.

Jean-Baptiste misread what the man was doing and growled at him: "Attends! Wait! Put that thing away! You'll get your turn. I don't want to be feeling any pressure to finish." He grinned his bobcat grin again. He turned to Second Son, "You say she hasn't been with a man yet?"

But Second Son, exhausted by his drunken struggle with Young Rabbit Woman, had already sat on the ground with his back to a tree, his eyes going crooked and blank.

Another of the men, a tall, broad bull with a big stomach said, "I'll not fuck her after you've been there, Le Putois! You think I want your slime on my cock? I'm next!" He pushed the one who had picked up Joe's gun—the one who was no longer wide-eyed but was now staring at Jean-Baptiste Bourque through slitted lids.

Le Putois jumped away from the big man's touch like a snake had struck him on the arm. They called him Paul Le Putois, Paul the Skunk, because he had a wide streak of white hair from the front of his head to the back where a man had tried to scalp him in a drinking house fight one time. He had tried to change the story to turn it into an attack by a pack of Iroquois, which would make him look like a big hero, but the truth was—and everybody knew it but they didn't dare say it in front of his face—that it was some crazy Portugais running from the law in Virginia, and who'd stowed away on a French ship on the home voyage by way of Port Royal, and who had been discovered there and put ashore scared to death and madder than hell. They'd both been drinking all day at the Port Royal inn when Paul Le Putois had made some comment to the Portugais about looking and acting like a frightened young girl when the little Portuguese man had exploded, jumped on the table, and started hacking away at the head of Paul Le Putois with a gutting knife he'd snatched out of the belt of the man he'd been standing beside. It took several men to pull him off the cursing Paul Le Putois to drag him outside. Normally, in a case like this, with a stranger attacking one of their own, the men would have given the stranger a good going over once they had him outside in the dark. But because nobody much liked Paul Le Putois, they just walked the Portugais far off into the bush and left him to his own drunken devices with a verbal warning that a man like Paul Le Putois was not one you wanted to make an enemy of even though he was usually the first one to disappear when a fight broke out, even if he'd been the one to start it.

Although Paul Le Putois wasn't as tough as he wanted to think he was—especially right then trying to stare down the biggest man in l'Acadie—he was often unpredictable so always got away with things by scowling his most menacing grimace at people who then backed down. But as he sat down he muttered something about not wanting to have the poor wretch of a girl in the first place. Yes, Paul Le Putois was something of a coward, but not ever to be an underestimated coward as the rotting body of the Portugais would attest to. It was found a few miles northeast of Port Royal several weeks after the fight, the scattered bones heavily scored by animal teeth. (But you could still tell that his throat had been slit so deep his head had almost fallen off.) There was a story went around for a while that someone had found a musket ball hole in the back of the Portuguese man's buckskin coat, but not many believed the story, saying not even Paul Le Putois could sink so low as to first shoot a man in the back to be able to slit his throat.

While this stare-down had been going on between Paul Le Putois and the tall, broad man appropriately called Le Gros (or, behind his back, La Grossesse, meaning "pregnancy"), Joe listened helplessly while the man he now recognized as Poissard (the masculine form of "Fish Wife") held the knife to his throat. He could smell alcohol among the other stinks on the man's breath and hoped the man was drunk enough that his reflexes were slowed down so Joe could jump free and grab the knife tucked into the leg wrappings on his left calf.

Joe knew that if he could get free long enough to get his knife out, he had an excellent chance against the man. Being left-handed made it sometimes difficult to learn skills from a right-handed teacher, but it gave a man an advantage in a fight because most men had learned to fight against right-handed opponents. Joe could see through the kaksk'ug that Young Rabbit Woman was beginning to stir slightly. Her foot moved. Joe saw it. The man holding the knife against Joe's throat saw it, too, and looked away for the space of two heartbeats, giving Joe time to slam the back of his left hand into Poissard's nose. Joe felt his knuckles connect, heard the *snik* of breaking cartilage, twisted free. His knife was already in his hand by the time he was facing Poissard. He lunged. Poissard dodged, cried out:

"Maudit! Tabernacle! Da son of a whore got away! Chalice! He busted by fucking doze! Get da fuck over here and help me kill the fucking asshole!"

"I'm busy," hollered Jean-Baptiste. "Go help him, Le Putois!"

"I'll get the gun," said Paul Le Putois as he scuttled across the clearing toward the coureurs de bois cabin under the trees.

"Chalice. You asshole," came Poissard's voice from inside the clump of kaksk'ug. "You don't need no fucking gun. Just yer knife. There's two on one, then. Saint sacrement, Le Putois, did your mother have any children with brains? Hurry, chalice!"

"Je viens, je viens. Keep your shirt on!" Paul Le Putois trudged slowly back across the clearing, his shaking hands trying to claw the knife out of the ragged leather scabbard hanging off his belt.

Behind him, Le Gros called out: "Hé! Le Putois! When's the last time you used that knife of yours? Stirring your baby porridge?"

"Ta goule! Shut up!"

Truth be told, not many of the men who lived on the rough side of the coureurs de bois life were very old. If you wanted to see your hair and your teeth falling out from old age and not from being punched, paddled or poisoned, pissing on people's good nature wherever you went was not the best way to do it. Some of them had taken up the lonely life of trapping because they couldn't stand the lonely life of civilization. Some of them were running from women, from the fathers of women, from lawmen, or from each other. On the rough side, all of them were at least a little bit crazy whether they had started out that way or not.

Paul Le Putois had not had it easy. His great-grandfather had been one of the Scots who was living at the fort when two of the Newcomers' Kings made a trade and the King in Claude's land got Acadia back. This meant everybody who wasn't French had to go back home to where he came from so the great-grandfather left. When his grandson, the father of Paul Le Putois, got himself into trouble—somebody said he killed a man—the grandfather and the father decided they could hide him in Nouvelle France, close to where the grandfather had lived. So they sent him (along with a great deal of money and under a false name) to the fort near our village. When things settled down and the grandfather had set things up to have another man hang for the murder their boy had committed, they told him it was safe for him to return. But the boy had caused so much trouble on the way over (and he'd only been fourteen at the time), that no captain would allow him to board his ship to get back home—nor would any ship's owner no matter how much money was waved under his nose. It wasn't just the drink made him mean, he just had a streak in him that was pure anger all the time. He could control it without the alcohol, but when he got drinking, he was a right terror to be around, for man and woman both. Ships' owners and captains—and even his own father, I heard—hoped the bush would get him; those who'd had the misfortune of doing any dealings with him here hoped a chenoo, a wendigo, would take him back home to his own land.

Not being able to go back to his land did not bother the man everybody was now calling The Scotsman. He had built himself a good business and had no one to answer to but himself. He liked this. If he'd gone back home, he would have been under the eye of both his father and grandfather and his father was as suppressive as his grandfather was lenient. Here, he was free to do whatever he pleased no matter what it was or to whom he did it. There was only one thing missing in his life: a son to carry on with what he had built up and he was now almost forty winters old and had never been able to convince any of the local women to marry him even though he had a house and had made a lot of money with the lumber up by Île Royale, the furs of course, and he had a lot of livestock that he sold to Newcomers or sold away. So he went to the settlement at Québec to get himself a woman there. If you had property and money, which he did, you could get yourself a wife by wooing her (that is, her parents) for a moon or two and by answering their questions the way you thought they wanted to hear them answered. Money and influence and lies could work miracles he was often heard to say.

Within three moons The Scotsman was back with a wife all trained in the fine points like running a household (although he dismissed all the servants the moment he brought her into his house), and etiquette (although they never went anywhere or had any visitors to speak of), and with a lot of money (although that was now in his hands). He allowed her to bring back several trunks full of womanly items like a velvet-lined box that had once belonged to Gabrielle d'Estrées, mistress of Henry IV of France and it wasn't long before The Scotsman had chopped up her velvet-lined box for firewood and had her working, pregnant or not, behind a horse in the fields while he sat on a rock and told her how she was doing it all wrong and making her start over, time and again.

She came to the mother of One-Eyed Joe one time—that's how we all found out—and told her that she wanted, needed to get back to Québec because the man was going to end up killing her he was so insanely jealous. The mother of One-Eyed Joe made a big mistake then. She was so angry when the young French girl showed her the welts on her back and the bump on her left arm where the break hadn't healed properly, that she took off to where Paul Le Putois's father was and screeched at him like a fisher cat until some of our people went there and pulled her off him and took her back to her wikuom.

I said it was a mistake because the father of Paul Le Putois took his young wife and baby, Paul, away with him to Île Royale and the lumber camps, where he lived so far back in the bush, nobody could find them unless he wanted them to.

The population of people in those days wasn't as much as it is now, and there was a lot of activity among the coureurs de bois who seemed to go everywhere there was money to be made, so stories of The Scotsman and his sad, frightened wife and young son went around a lot. Some of the coureurs de bois came back with stories about loggers hearing screams when they worked up near Île Royale. In some places in that part of the country, the people say that the way the hills and valleys fit together you can hear a moose pass gas from a full day's journey away; but in other parts, a wolf can growl right beside you and you can't hear a thing. And they also say that some parts of that land make a man grow mean if he's bent that way in the first place.

Eventually, the logging spread to where The Scotsman and his family were living, except it was only the boy and his mother that were there. It would have been about five years since they left our village, and the loggers who found them said that the boy, young Paul, had eyes on him the size of an owl's when the men first entered the clearing at their cabin. The woman was not much better, they said; you could smell the stink of fear on her and they knew right away it must have been her making that terrible screaming over the years. But when they thought about it, they realized they hadn't heard the screaming for more than a few weeks now.

When they asked where The Scotsman was, the boy covered his head with his hands and ran away into the cabin. The woman just said: "Mort. Dead."

She was brought back to our village in the spring of the following year, and to us she didn't seem as bad as the stories had made her out to be, although her face was crooked and her teeth were broken and she walked hunched over a bit. But she seemed happy enough. It was the boy, now six winters old, who jumped every time somebody said anything to him, and his eyes truly did look like an owl's, wide and staring and not moving except when he moved his head.

Once again it was the mother of One-Eyed Joe who got the story out of the mother of Paul Le Putois. Some of the story, at least. The young woman wanted to forget most of it. But she ended up telling the mother of One-Eyed Joe about the boy's dreams of his dead father rolling the stones off his grave to reach out with merciless hands to punch, crush and grind his face like he had done to his mother's. Young Paul's nightmares were terrible, said his mother, and she could do nothing to stop them or help the child when he would wake every single night crying out like he was dying because he believed his father was coming out of the grave to kill him. She had tried over and over, she said, to explain to her child about death-stiffness, because when they were burying the man, still stiff from recent death, she had bent his arms with great difficulty to fold them over his chest, and tied them with a bit of yarn she used to do her mending. Then she and her son had begun to pile round smooth stones on top of the body. They had finished the chore and were sitting, no, she said, kneeling beside the grave to say une petite prière, a little prayer, for the soul of her husband, when the rocks started to move and one of them tumbled down as his death-stiff arm shot out and struck Paul on the neck.

"How did he die?" asked the mother of One-Eyed Joe.

"Me and the boy," answered the young woman. "We killed him. We took sticks when he was passed out drunk in the shed and we killed him. We hit and hit and hit his head until his brains came out. Then we left him until the morning when we heard voices through the trees and thought the loggers were close, but it was only the echoes of the bush we heard, but we drug his body out to the field too soon anyways where the rocks were most plentiful and we dug as deep as we could with the plowshare then covered him up with stones." She took a deep breath, her head was bowed, and she began to sob in great whoops. "But they never… came… until… the next… month."

The mother of One-Eyed Joe took the wailing young woman into her arms and she told us the woman cried like that until the sun came up.

It helped her a lot to cry like that, the mother of One-Eyed Joe would tell you if you asked, but they could never do anything about the boy. He just grew up on his own and with his own ideas about stuff. And when he took up with the coureurs de bois, the people said, Well that's the end of him.

So when Paul Le Putois heard the sound of the woman's screams as Jean-Baptiste penetrated her, taking her virginity, Paul Le Putois panicked. In the meantime, Poissard (the masculine form of Fish Wife) continued to curse and scream, yelling "Help me! Saint sacrement. Chalice! Help me. M'aidez, tabernacle! Hostie. M'aidez. Help me kill this fucking Indian!"

Paul Le Putois ran up and said: "I can't help you right now but I'll even the fight for you, Poissard." And he grabbed Joe from behind and scraped his fish-gutty old knife across Joe's eyes, then he ran to where the screaming woman was. The screaming woman and Jean-Baptiste. Jean-Baptiste who was just this moment getting off her and cursing her because he came too fast.

Jean-Baptiste kicked her once on the bare buttocks and cursed her again. Drawing his leg back to aim for a second kick, he barely registered the sort of mewling sound that Paul Le Putois made when he cocked the gun.

Young Rabbit Woman says that was the last sound Jean-Baptiste Bourque ever heard.

Three

The year I was coming up to my fifteenth winter, as the summer wore on, it seemed that most days I found myself not visiting Claude Guidry as often as I usually did. I always hated it when he left abruptly after the first heavy frost so I guess I was trying to wean myself off him like Orignal-Sale weaned her piglets off of her. I kept myself busy learning new ways now that I was no longer a child. I took over many of my mother's tasks so she could spend more time preparing and drying sweetgrass and making pemmican. (Many said that my mother's pemmican had a special spirit nature in it because of the strength it gave them when they ate it.) And, of course, I helped the mother of One-Eyed Joe collect the plants, berries, bark, roots and seeds we needed to heal people who had been injured or who had a sickness. And I learned almost too much to fit inside my head from the Grandfathers that summer, too. So I was surprised this particular year to see Claude Guidry staying on his compound this late in the fall—he usually spent most of his time between first and last frost laying and checking his traps in the bush—but then I remembered that in the Rabbit Cycle this was the year of disease for them. We wouldn't eat them like that and their fur was uneven and dull, therefore useless. Until the foxes and wolves cleaned out the sick ones and the others started having healthy young, it wasn't a good idea to cut down their numbers even further by going out on the land for nothing but your own greed. Rabbits were usually plentiful and easy to catch and the young ones skinned up fast and cooked up tender; you used the older ones for fur. Without a lot of good rabbits around, a long journey wasn't a wise thing to do unless you had to. A lot of the coureurs de bois—the French ones—did not respect our ways and went trapping anyway during the disease year of the Rabbit Cycle. All they wanted to do was make money and didn't care much for the future of the trade as long as they could trade for their supplies today. Claude Guidry was more like our people. For one thing, he never traded furs for alcohol or alcohol for furs like the other French Runners did. The other French Runners didn't care if the rabbit meat they ate was wormy or had sores because they would just wash it down with alcohol anyway, laughing and trying to teach our people that alcohol cures every disease.

Claude Guidry—he told me his name used to have an accent aigu on an e to make it Guédry—came from what he laughingly called bon élevage, good breeding. He was telling me this story as we helped his pig, Orignal-Sale, farrow her latest litter of piglets, so I also thought it was a funny expression. His grandfather had been a successful shipping business owner in England until he emigrated with the family to France and became even more successful as the middleman between the Ivory Coast traders and the English ivory shippers. (Claude explained to me that "even more successful" meant "even richer.") Claude's father, the eldest, was thirteen when the family moved to France and his name was changed from John to Jean. The family's last name remained Guildry, a proud name signifying many generations of Masonic English Cutler Guildsmen. When Claude's father married a woman from a prominent French family, his last name (on his new wife's family's insistence) became Guédry, with the accent; and his religion (to Claude's grandmother's horror) became Roman Catholicism.

After Claude's father, Jean, passed away, Claude's two older brothers, Will and Henri, had taken over the business and, according to Claude, would eventually be the ruination of it trucking with Dutch and Portuguese slave traders like they were still doing.

"My grandfather always said 'Leave the slaves to the Dutch and the Portuguese as they alone have the stomach for it.' Grandfather tried it once in defiance of his own father with one shipload to the Indies," said Claude. "But the winds did not favor this voyage. He lost most of them to starvation and disease. This completely sickened him against the slave trade as he never thought of these creatures as being anything less than human. Not like the Portuguese. So he went back home, ashamed of himself and determined to continue providing ivory to the Cutler Company of London as his family had done for generations.

"Eventually, however, an Act of Parliament in 1624 allowed the establishment of the 'Company of Cutlers in Hallamshire' in Sheffield. Grandfather thought the Hallamshire Master Cutler was a crook and a traitor, so he refused to do direct business with him and went so far as to move his business clear out of the country.

"It was better to do his business from France to Africa and back as middleman," Claude said. "Fewer risks. More profit. Less intrigue."

I really liked my friend Claude Guidry because he explained everything about his life and his people and answered my every question with patience and never looked at me as if I was stupid when I interrupted his stories. Not like the Father at all.

When I would ask the Father things like why Jesus picked only men to follow him, and asked if that meant that Jesus was womanly, what we called two-spirited—something revered by our people—he would become angry and tell me to be quiet and say my prayers, that I should not say such terrible things about Jesus or I would go to hell for sure. It sounded to me like the words he was putting into everybody's ears were coming out of Feather's mouth the same way they went in. This made me wonder—all the time—what kind of magic the Father had used on her, and on others of our people. I was also wondering if the Father thought Mi'gmaw girls and women shouldn't learn anything except what he wanted to stuff our heads with, most of which was pure nonsense. For instance, I heard two very different stories about what happened to Claude after his arrival in Virginia: one story from the Father and one story from Claude. The parts of the stories that were the same frightened me half to death wondering how Claude had managed to escape with his life.

Four

Claude had come in the *Perroquet*, one of his brothers' slave ships that had come directly from the Ivory Coast to Haiti where they dropped off their living cargo, then on to Jamestown, Virginia, for the cotton the people in Brittany wanted. Claude said he hated Jamestown and called it un monde barbare. He said the people there were civilized on the front, especially the ladies, but behind their cordialité was a knife at your back if you were not English. To them, everyone was a pirate and a spy. Claude was neither but they still treated him like he was.

Except for the difference in the way the sails were made, the *Perroquet* was exactly like the ships owned by the Dutch, the Portuguese and the Spanish—usually French-built for shipping cloth, guns, rum and sugar but not what they called "live cargo." The *Perroquet* was one of the first to begin using the ocean's currents to make for quick and easy sailing from France to the Ivory Coast, to the Indies, then back to France, selling and buying goods at each point along the way. The profits were enormous, and Claude often said he had to at least give his brothers credit for having the brains to use the ocean like that.

At first Claude didn't want to tell me why he left Saint-Malo, but eventually I learned that a woman was behind his decision. As I look back from now, it appears that all Claude's decisions in life were because of women. Like I said before, it wouldn't surprise me if Claude Guidry had a woman at the end of every day's journey, and I don't think it was just me who had that opinion. The girls and the women in both communities, Mi'gmaw and French, couldn't take their eyes off him whenever he walked by.

He was taller than I and I was taller than most of the Mi'gmaw men in my village and all the women except for my older sister. I already told you about his amazing green eyes. His skin was darker than most of the other French men and darker than mine in the summer but I wasn't as dark as some of our people but darker than others. When I asked him why his skin was so nice and brown, he laughed and told me the story of one of his uncles' wives who had called his mother's mother a maudit Hindou in a fit of drunken rage one time. And when he explained that one of his ancestors had owned Hindu slaves and that one of them had taken a real fancy to the wife of this owner (his grandmother), and that the slave's owner had sold the man shortly after the wife's daughter had been born, I laughed along with him. Our people had stories like that, too. They weren't funny if it happened to you, but they were plenty funny if they happened to somebody else. The family always said it wasn't true, but once you plant the seed of doubt in anyone's mind, it will grow there whether you water it or not.

So the ingredients that created Claude Guidry were French and English blood with a suspicion of "maudit Hindou" thrown in for good measure. It was no wonder women couldn't keep their eyes, nor—I soon discovered—their hands off him.

He came to Jamestown, Virginia, off his brothers' ship nearly a year before he stumbled out of the bush into our village wearing the worst kind of clothing for the bush you could ever wear. At first, my people thought he must have been one of the angels the priests talked about. Anyone who could survive the bush after such a long journey wearing clothes like that had to have powerful magic of some kind working for them, so they called him La Verdure, the Woodsman.

There had been a woman on the ship, the fiancée of Peter Wingfield, distant cousin of the late Edward Maria Wingfield, deposed Roman Catholic first president of the colony. (I got that part of the story from Father Soucy first because of the Roman Catholic connection. And that part was true.) Her name was Sarah Rolfe and she had clapped eyes on Claude Guidry and that was the end of her betrothal to the likes of Peter Wingfield as far as she was concerned. But not as far as Peter Wingfield was concerned. This put Claude in what he called une situation précaire, a precarious position, so once again, Claude was forced to flee from a woman's love. (That part? I think it was true, too.) But maybe I'm getting ahead of my story. I should really start by telling you about Madame, shouldn't I?

☽ ○ ☾

Claude was eighteen years old when Madame Louise first noticed him standing beside his father and his eldest brother, Will, at her elaborate New Year's Eve *balle* held at her husband's Saint-Malo estate. Their families were neighbors—if you can call people living three leagues from front gate to front gate, neighbors. The new year would be 1666 and her husband, Philibert de Villegaignon, Marquis de Savoie, had just announced he would be financially backing Nicolas Grévin and three ships to explore the Galápagos Islands. Philibert had announced as well—to Madame's surprise but not to her dismay—that he would be accompanying Monsieur Grévin on the voyage.

Claude's brother, Will, nudged his arm saying: "Merde. She's heading over here. Be careful, little brother. She's a spider."

Before Claude could react, Will had disappeared through the elaborate glass doors behind him and a beautiful young woman had latched onto Claude's other arm, her face a mere foot from his. "Pray tell me your name," she purred.

A purring spider? Claude thought. What a dangerous beast that makes. He could feel the blood rising up his neck to his ears and this made him blush further as he stammered: "Claude Guédry, son of Jean—"

"And brother of Will who has fled the room." Her voice was sweet, her gaze direct, demanding. He could smell réglisse, liquorice, on her breath. She stepped away from him so her eyes could more easily travel from his toes to his head and back again, lingering at mid-ships during both voyages.

"Puis, uh. Oui. Yes, Madame."

"No need to be shy with me, my dear Claude. Won't you take my arm for this dance?"

Claude clicked his heels together, bowing slightly. "Avec plaisir, Madame." And he extended his arm for her, but her fingers had already curled again around his forearm. She moved smoothly beside him as though she were on strings. *A spider indeed.*

"I see your mother has chosen to hurt my feelings yet again by not attending my party."

"I'm sorry, Madame," he said now placing his right hand at her waist to direct her. He was surprised at how tiny her waist was, and that it was unencumbered by a corset. "Maman had a previous commitment and was unable to attend. My father extended her regrets, did he not?"

"Indeed he did. But he's plein de merde, full of shit." She laughed as she twirled away to take the hand of the next man in line in the dance.

The young woman whose hand Claude took—she was about fourteen, he thought—glanced up once at his face and said: "I did hear right, didn't I? She did say that, didn't she?" And the girl began to giggle as

Claude handed her back to her partner and took Madame's hand back into his own.

"What did that annoying brat say to you, my dear Claude? She's my husband's niece and at the request of his sister, he's been trying to marry her off to royalty. I'm trying to marry her off to anything! She's only been with us for seven months—a very long seven months! She's such a little twit. She follows me everywhere. I'm sure I'll go clean out of my mind when my husband leaves for the Galápagos Islands and I am stuck entertaining her all by myself. I can't wait to get her married off. A friend of mine has a son who seems absolutely smitten with her, but he's awfully young to take on the responsibilities of marriage. But perhaps a betrothal would get her off my hands until Philibert's return."

"She seems nice enough," said Claude.

"Mon dieu, my dear boy! It's obvious to me you've not spent much time entertaining young ladies or you would certainly know her type immediately."

"Oui, Madame. My apologies."

"Oh, look there," she said. "I must speak to the gentleman talking with my husband. Would you walk me over please?"

"Most certainly." He bowed, clicked his heels, and extended his arm once again to Madame.

"And the next time we meet," she whispered as they glided over to where her husband stood talking with a group of men. "You must drop the Madame and call me by my name which is Louise."

"Oui, Madame."

☽ ○ ☾

It wasn't long before Claude heard from Madame Louise. Within a week there was a messenger at the door placing an elaborately monogrammed and heavily perfumed letter of invitation into Claude's hand.

"Her said it had to be into his own hand, monsieur," exclaimed the messenger. "I am apologetic profoundly to make him stop his activities to come direct to the door, monsieur."

From a dish on the guéridon beside the front door, Claude extracted a sou to place into the messenger's gloved hand. "C'est propre. You did what Madame asked of you." He was closing the door when the messenger cleared his throat and said:

"I must to wait for la réponse monsieur. Or Madame will skin me alive, her said."

Claude told the man to wait outside and before cracking the letter's seal, he stepped into the library, closing the door.

> *Mon cher Claude. Urgent I see you. Come to supper Friday evening as escort to a dear lady friend of mine. Also, my husband's twit of a niece whom you met at the New Year's Balle will be there as will her young admirer. (I want your advice on him!) I have told the messenger to wait for the answer which must be yes!*

Claude told me that even though he was put off by the manners of this woman—or more by the lack of them—his curiosity toward Madame Louise was so strong that he quickly grabbed a sheet of paper bearing his family's Elephant and Castle crest, and dipping his pen into a bottle of ink, he wrote: Yes.

He remembered his brother's warning that she was… What had he called her? A spider? What an interesting thing to call a woman as beautiful as Madame. And how intriguing that his brother appeared to have intimate knowledge of her character. Friday's supper party was only two evenings away—when Claude hoped to discover on his own if she were a purring spider or a purring kitten transformed into a woman by a spell. But by a spell cast on her? Or by a spell cast on him?

☽ ○ ☾

If I hadn't trusted Claude Guidry as much as I did, I would not have believed a word he told me about the supper party Madame had invited him to. I had never even heard of (nor could have imagined) some of the food they presented at that meal. To tell you the truth, I don't think I would have had the stomach to eat much of anything they served. It didn't sound healthy to me at all. A lot of it wasn't even freshly killed but had sat in puddles of what Claude called "marinades" for a whole day or more. One-Eyed Joe's woman had cooked foreign meals for the Fathers, but she never told us about any of this. *This* was supposed to be "the latest thing" in France because it was the way Claude's King liked it. (Well, I think—I don't want to be rude of course—but I think if Claude's King liked it, he could have it.)

Claude explained to me that Louis the 14th, the King of France (France is the land Claude came from) had discovered a new way of cooking. It was invented by a man named La Varenne, and because the King liked it, it became the fashion for all the rich people in France. And because the rich people in France liked it, the rich people in many other places decided they would like it as well.

I didn't know that much about Kings. I only knew about Lnu Saqamaq which Claude said weren't the same thing at all. Claude explained that a King is a powerful man who owns everything in his country and sometimes in other people's countries, too. Except for God, he is Supreme Ruler over everyone. If somebody does something bad against him and he wants them killed for it, he just tells somebody to kill them. And he gets to be King because he was the first boy born in a King's family. You can have a Queen in a country, but Kings are better. Claude also explained that despite the impression King Louis was under, a Pope was better than a King and that's why we were supposed to listen to the Fathers. This last thing made me wonder about Claude: If he was telling me that people had to listen to the Fathers, why didn't he go to Mass all the time like Father Soucy kept yelling at all of us to do?

Claude then told me that King Louis the 14th was the owner of Acadia and that a Chief of the Fathers—his name was Bishop Laval—ran things over here for the Pope.

Like I said, I always trusted Claude to tell me what was true. I could see the part about the Fathers and their Chief running things. They were domineering enough. But this thing about King Louis *owning* the land? That was the strangest thing he ever told me. I thought Claude was telling me one of his jokes and I started laughing so hard water spilled out of my eyes, but when he got angry at me for laughing I stopped right away. I didn't stop because I believed this strange story about somebody owning the land, I stopped because my friend Claude believed it.

So when he told me how much food they served at Madame's dinners, I wasn't sure if he was telling me the truth or not. And I still wonder to this day what an amazing race of people they must be to be able to eat that many days' food at one meal. It would seem that Frenchmen were even stranger than anyone could have imagined when they first came here.

Claude told me that after Madame Louise's husband left for the Galápagos, the meals were not such a big production as before, so at first he thought it was Philibert, the Marquis who had been trying to put on the big show.

"It was only the Marquis who wanted the feast to be good?" I asked.

"For the most part it was he," Claude said. Then he started blushing which set me off to laughing again because I knew exactly what he was trying to cover up.

"Madame didn't want all those servants around, did she?" I said and got a big scowl out of him for it. But he nodded his head to agree anyway.

"They had a bigger dining room than we had at our estate," said Claude. "It was about ten feet longer, but about the same width. My suspicions were later confirmed by my brother, Will, that the Marquis was a social climber of the highest degree. He wasn't even a real marquis but had obtained his title—no one seemed to know how—several years earlier and had been trying to prove his worth ever since.

"Madame Louise had just as humble beginnings as the Marquis himself did so they were constantly trying to better themselves. Where the Marquis's money had come from no one seemed to know. Some had their suspicions. My brother at first thought perhaps the slave trade was the source. But no one had heard of the man doing any of that kind of business, and my brother was someone who had a lot of contacts regarding the slave trade. Anyone you spoke to, if they knew him at all, was of the opinion that his vast wealth had come from less-than-honorable sources. He said he had known the King but if he were to tell someone that the King had known him he would have been scorned by everyone as a complete liar. People who had known him when he lived in Versailles said he had often been seen among the crowd of courtiers when the King made his Promenades and that that was the closest Philibert de Villegaignon, Marquis de Savoie ever got to the King. But to hear Philibert speak, he had been a constant and important facet of the King's court. However, among those who were familiar with what was presented at the King's meals as well as at the meals of the Marquis, there were some wondered how the Marquis could know details of the King's private suppers in such intimacy, that perhaps there was some truth to the Marquis's words. But others said Philibert's sister was one of the King's mistresses; others said it was the sister of Madame Louise who was the mistress. Some said it was Madame Louise herself who had been a mistress of the King."

I asked why the Marquis and Madame Louise would feel they had to impress people who obviously didn't like them and Claude explained that if you come into the world in humble circumstances and start working your way up through the classes, objects and the owning of objects—mostly showing them off—will soon begin to take on a great deal of importance in your life. These objects, Claude said, begin to have a symbolism to them, a symbolism proving that you no longer have to worry about where your next bite of food is coming from. Eventually, you don't have to worry about anything anymore except trying to obtain and maintain people's respect. An impossible undertaking, of course: If you come up like that, people who knew you along the way always remember where you used to be and they'll still think of you as being that same person, only with money.

When I disagreed with Claude that you could not possibly be the same person if you started out with nothing and you worked really hard and ended up with a lot, he said: "You don't know how things are done in France, Keskoua. You can't move up from class to class like that. It just isn't done!"

"But Madame and the Marquis did it!" I argued.

"They fooled us. They weren't really who they said they were. The Marquis—Philibert—attained his title by underhanded means! It just isn't done. So leave it at that!"

I still wasn't satisfied but decided to let it go for now so Claude would get on with the story of how these people could eat so much without bursting or throwing everything up, or worse. I know if I ate too much rice sometimes, I would spend all the next day digging holes in the bush.

"I remember the first meal well," Claude began. "It was such a big production, and so very different from the way our family ate, who could forget it?

"Because there were only six of us: Madame Louise at the foot, then myself to the right of her, then one of Madame's lady friends, Philibert, the friend's thirteen-year-old son, and of course Véronique, the niece of Philibert. The servants had set up an impressive table for us to eat at. I can't recall the lady friend's name, nor that of the son—a rather bookish, pale sort. It appeared to me that he was totally besotted with young Véronique who at first seemed to encourage him, then turned her attention to myself." Claude laughed and added: "If he'd been older, I think I would have feared for my continued good health as his eyes were shooting such daggers at me through those spectacles of his."

I just shook my head. I think this was when I first knew for sure that women were never anything else but trouble for Claude. "Forget that!" I demanded. "Tell me about the feast."

"They put most of the dishes on a sideboard from which the servants then filled our plates. There were more than fifty dishes brought in, held high on the shoulders of as many servants. As I told you, Philibert and Madame Louise did many things the same way King Louis did at Versailles, but on a much less grand scale, of course.

"There were four variations of soup to start, and Madame would not be satisfied until all of us had tried each of them. The partridge with cabbage was excellent, and the pigeon and capon soups not much more than thin broth with a few vegetables. For the life of me, though, I could not bring myself to dip my spoon into the soup with the pieces of cockscomb and wattles floating in it. Véronique and Philibert both said it was delicious, but I was still getting used to these new culinary forms and dared not risk making myself ill the first time visiting someone.

"I attempted to parry the attention away from my soup toward the latest news of the day by mentioning the death a few weeks earlier of Catherine de Vivonne, Marquise de Rambouillet.

"Young Véronique, noticing my distress, jumped in to save me from my embarrassment.

"'Ah, oui,' she said. 'What will Molière ever write about now that Madame de Rambouillet is gone?'

"'Mais, he stopped writing about that crowd years ago,' interjected Philibert. 'After his friend Fouquet went to prison for having him perform *Les Fâcheux* during that scandalously expensive series of parties thrown in the King's honor, I don't think Molière would dare remind the King of those silly women and their even sillier companions. I mean really! They were popular plays I must admit—not to mention extremely funny—but they were expensive, too. Obviously, with Colbert running things now as Finance Minister—and since he was the one ultimately behind Fouquet's disgrace—I'd be surprised if we ever see another play by Monsieur Molière.'

"'My dear husband,' laughed Madame Louise. 'You can't blame Fouquet's downfall on Molière's play! It was that ballet-dancing Italian sodomite Lully behind Fouquet's falling out of favor with the King. The King adores Lully! So by association then, he has to adore Molière's plays for which Lully writes the music. It only makes the greatest of sense. Especially since they are all in it together with your Jean-Baptiste Colbert. Even you cannot deny that Colbert had his eye on the position of Finance Minister ever since he came to court.'

"I had by this time managed to touch my napkin to my lips and nudge aside the plate of soup in which floated those foul-looking pieces of fowl. From somewhere behind me, one of the servants slipped his arm past me to remove the offending plate from my sight. I looked over at Véronique who winked at me and smiled. I would be forever grateful to young Véronique for saving *ma face*, my face, on this occasion and for saving *ma fesse*, my rear end, on another.

"The rest of the meal was vastly more than tolerable but since I was still used to the old way of using many spices to mask the odor of food, tasting the real meat—although with under-flavorings of this and that—

was perplexing if not unnerving at times. As I put each bite into my mouth I half expected to detect that usual off-odor that was so often beneath what I was used to eating. I must admit that the chicken with truffles was deliciously beyond what I imagined it would be just by looking at it.

"Keep in mind, Keskoua, that King Louis is inspired in his development of so many new ideas."

"What did his sweat lodges look like?" I asked. "Did he build them in his gardens at Versailles? Or did he build them when he was away from Versailles at his other places?"

Five

I told you already that I stopped flirting with Father Soucy, but I think maybe he missed me doing that because now he always stopped me to say stuff when I walked by, like: How have you been? I see you sit in the back of the church at Mass now. You only go to Mass on Sundays. I see you spend a lot of time at Claude Guidry's compound. You shouldn't spend time alone with a grown man who doesn't go to Mass regularly. I see you being with Young Rabbit Woman a lot. More than you're with young people your own age. He would always frown and click his tongue when he said this last part because after the bad thing happened to Young Rabbit Woman, who was twelve winters older than me, she stopped going to the Father's to make his meals and clean his house. And she stopped going to Mass, too.

Father Soucy wanted me to still be friends with Hélène—dear sweet Feathery Hélène! even though she was two winters older—because her Mass attendance was good, he said. But I think it was really because she believed him that our ways were bad.

The one who was making the Father's meals and cleaning his house now was The Scotsman's wife, the mother of Paul Le Putois. Her name was Geneviève and she had come from the settlement at Québec, so although she lived in our village with us, she was more like the Father in one way: they were both Frenchmen.

She never went to the fort not even for flour. One of the Grandmothers told me that Geneviève couldn't bring herself to look at a White man ever again. The Father didn't count because he was a priest.

"But it wasn't all White men who hurt The Scotsman's wife," I said. I wasn't sure I liked her because Claude Guidry always watched her when she was walking past. "Doesn't she trust any of them? Her face is scarred and ugly, but she's not old. She could marry again and have a husband to hunt for her and feed her and not always have to make our women share."

After I said that about Geneviève, the Grandmother's face looked sad even though she was smiling at me when she said: "I hope and pray, young Keskoua, that you never learn what it's like to be at the hands of a bad man."

Maybe that's what caused the bad medicine to come against me later.

☽ ○ ☾

I suppose you might be wondering what happened to everybody after Paul Le Putois shot Jean-Baptiste Bourque in the back out at Mouse Ridge when he finished fucking Young Rabbit Woman and started kicking her because he came too fast.

Because Second Son was passed out drunk he missed the whole thing. In fact he never even remembered how he got to Mouse Ridge or why he went there.

Joe's right eye was ruined after Paul Le Putois had slashed his knife across it, and his left eye had a scratch on it so he wasn't exactly seeing straight if he was even looking at anything right then anyway. He says he heard the shot.

Poissard was still hopping around in the kaksk'ug, the cedars, with blood running into his mouth from his broken nose, and still cursing anything to do with the Mass. He says he didn't hear anything.

Le Gros says he didn't hear anything, he didn't see anything, and he wasn't even there.

Paul Le Putois disappeared.

Nobody asked Young Rabbit Woman.

According to the Pamphlet of Regulations for soldiers stationed at the fort, Relations With Indian Women were forbidden. By extension (although it never stopped anybody), the other Frenchmen weren't supposed to get involved with us either, so the whole matter was dropped. It didn't take an extra-smart person to see that all of us, the soldiers, the coureurs de bois, the French who lived at the fort, and the Mi'gmaq alike, were glad to be rid of Jean-Baptiste Bourque. Still, it was best for Paul Le Putois to stay hidden for as long as he could.

I know that Young Rabbit Woman took food out to him for many winters. I caught her sneaking through the trees with a food sack one time, and although I asked her outright if the food was for Paul Le Putois, she smiled and didn't answer me. I wanted to know if his eyes were still like owl's eyes and if he had bad dreams about Jean-Baptiste Bourque now along with the bad dreams about his father coming out from under the grave stones to get him. I know she wanted to tell me, but she still wouldn't say. I thought maybe she was afraid I would tell Claude Guidry and that he might tell someone at the fort; that maybe the whole issue might get dredged up again even after ten summers; and that they'd want to find Paul Le Putois and hang him. They changed soldiers every three summers and the new ones wouldn't know what Jean-Baptiste Bourque had been like.

Geneviève, Paul Le Putois's mother, used to bring him food, too, and she also made clothing for him secretly and tried to decorate it like we did. She told me the real reason Young Rabbit Woman was afraid to tell anyone: It was because of what Paul Le Putois had done to Joe's eye. After all, Young Rabbit Woman was Joe's woman.

Of course, One-Eyed Joe knew all along that his woman was bringing food to the man who had half-blinded him, but Joe also understood why, so he never said anything until one spring when Poissard opened his foul, offensive mouth and shouted, in front of the whole village:

"Hé! One-Eye! Saint sacrement! I seen your fucking woman with Paul the Skunk last week out in the bush. What's the matter, chalice? Can't keep her satisfied?"

Poissard, like drunks tend to do, was still holding onto his anger over getting his nose broken by Joe that time so whenever their paths crossed, Poissard would try to start something with One-Eyed Joe. Joe never got pulled into these situations, but this time I could see his jaw clench and if I hadn't known Joe as well as I did, I would have been scared of him right then. To save face, Joe had to pretend to stop Young Rabbit Woman from taking any more food out to Paul Le Putois so he forbade her in front of everybody, but secretly, he allowed it because he knew it made her feel good—but only on the days he went out on the land to check his traps or to hunt or fish.

Because Geneviève found it so hard to walk through the bush with her bad back—remember I said she was bent over a bit?—she wasn't able to take stuff out to her son very often to fill in for the days Young Rabbit Woman couldn't, so Paul Le Putois started sneaking in to where the Father lived just outside our village. Sometimes Paul Le Putois even slept in the woodshed behind the church.

I don't think I have to tell you that eventually pretty well everybody figured out that Paul Le Putois was slinking around the village now. Everybody but the Father, that is. I guess if you spend your life teaching people that their ways are bad, you can't exactly use their ways to notice maybe some things were out of place. Some things even the youngest

Mi'gmaw could see with his eyes covered: Like footprints, for instance, or empty food bowls sitting there beside the woodshed, or your supplies were getting used up faster than you were using them yourself.

If the Father had known that Paul Le Putois was around that often, I'm pretty sure things would have turned out much differently for me. For the Father, too.

☽ ○ ☾

Geneviève told Young Rabbit Woman and she told me that after Paul Le Putois shot Jean-Baptiste Bourque in the back, his nightmares stopped and he changed. He stopped drinking alcohol for one thing, she said. I don't know if she was trying to get us to make friends with him and welcome him into our village as one of us (which we were reluctant to do); or if she was just trying to convince herself that her son was normal (which he could never be). The furthest any of us would go was what Young Rabbit Woman was doing which was bring food out to him, and what One-Eyed Joe did which was let her do it.

I never actually saw him but I could feel him watching me sometimes when I was on the way back to the village from Claude's or from the fort and walking past the wooden church and the Father's wooden house. I would just catch a movement in the corner of my eye but if I looked, there would be nothing there, not even a leaf moving. Sometimes it was a shift of something near the woodpile, or an extra shadow beside one of the snawe'g, or maybe nothing but a feeling. Maybe I should have been frightened of him but I wasn't for some reason. Did I think it was because I heard he had changed? That he wasn't drinking? No. I still didn't trust him after what he did to One-Eyed Joe even though it was a long time ago, and what he had done to Jean-Baptiste Bourque for hurting Young Rabbit Woman, but he didn't scare me. Had I picked something up from one of the Father's talks about "forgiving one's enemies"? That would be the last thing because Paul Le Putois wasn't my enemy and I didn't believe anything that ever came out of the Father's mouth anymore after he had turned my Feathery Hélène against our ways and our people. Paul Le Putois never did anything to me his whole life except look at me when I was little with those terribly terrified owl eyes. He scared me then. It was like nobody was living in behind those eyes of his and he just walked around the village as if he wasn't seeing anything or even thinking anything. At the time I thought that was probably why he never learned from our people when he was young how to hunt for food and cook it. He watched them do stuff, but he was never really in there to remember what he saw. I was glad when he came of age and left the village to run the woods. Some of our older people were saying he should be banished anyway because he caused bad medicine to happen, like one time we had three bad years in a row in a Rabbit Cycle.

Somehow he learned to trap, though. He was good at trapping and even better than some of us at those all-important first stages of hide preparation. He was even able to get the brains out of a moose skull without getting it all scratched up, and he had a special knack for telling just how much brains to put in the pot to cure a certain size of skin. At one time he made a lot of money with hides. He did learn how to hunt but he couldn't even look at food if it was cut up before it got to his plate. That's why he always went onto the land with a group of coureurs de bois. As long as one of them could cook the way he needed his food done up he was fine. After he had disappeared into the bush pretending he didn't exist anymore, he wasn't able, of course, to sell any of his furs or follow any runners who would cook the special way for him, so like a child, he became dependent on women to make his food and bring it to him.

There wasn't any one of us who was able to get right into Paul Le Putois's head to see what happened in there when he tried to prepare food for himself, but the mother of One-Eyed Joe, who was pretty old by now, had seen enough summers and winters and Newcomers to be able to explain some of it to me. She told me most of the story the day she taught me how to peel strips off a swamp ash log for making baskets.

"They aren't like us," she said. I said something like that was no surprise to me and she told me if I wanted to hear the story of Paul Le Putois I should shut up and listen. "You want to be a storyteller, don't you?" She made sure I nodded yes before she continued. Some of these older people were really good at making you feel ashamed of yourself. It's a good job they weren't priests or *nobody* would believe in our ways anymore.

At first she was surprised, she said, when she heard he was able to handle brains of any kind after what he and his mother had done to his father The Scotsman, beating the brains out of his head like that. She also thought that maybe that was the reason he was so good at it. If you change something terrible in your life just a little bit and then keep doing it over and over, it can help you forget the terrible thing because you start to believe that the new thing is actually the same as the old one.

"Sounds awful complicated. I don't think I could make myself forget if something terrible happened to me."

"Keskoua…"

"All right. I know. Be quiet."

At first she didn't want to tell me why Paul Le Putois had a problem with preparing food for himself. It was only meat, she explained. Only meat. He was able to gather berries and cook corn and stuff like that, but he couldn't do the meat. And he wouldn't eat pemmican at all because of the little bits of things in it. According to his mother, even when Paul Le Putois became a youth, he would still run away screaming any time someone offered him a piece of pemmican.

"You sure you want me to keep telling this story?" asked the mother of One-Eyed Joe. "It's not like anything our people have ever done. And I don't know if it's true or not, but I heard it happens sometimes with the people in the North. Careful with that! You'll split it. Take your time."

"My fingers are getting sore."

"You're not a small child anymore, Keskoua. You have to learn to do these things. I'm surprised your mother hasn't taught you how to make baskets."

I must have looked at her funny or something because she said: "Ah. Little Miss Keskoua is too smart now that she's coming up to fifteen winters to learn something from her mother, is she?"

"Tell me the rest of the story."

"Don't blame me if you never again eat meat." She thought that was funny and so did I when she said it, but for the rest of that day I ate only corn and berries—and no pemmican for a whole moon after.

The Scotsman was always saying his wife Geneviève was fooling around with the loggers even though the loggers were never within miles of their cabin. I told you that some places in the bush had echoes you could hear forever. He would tell her he heard their voices talking and then he would beat her until she fell down unconscious. Sometimes she wouldn't wake up for a whole day.

We're always hearing stories about woodsmen and coureurs de bois getting lost or going missing in the bush and never being found or showing up again. The men who worked these jobs knew the dangers and if they slipped up and made a mistake, they pretty well knew that their own death would be on their own head. But there was one man who didn't get lost so much as he "disappeared" one day. When we use the word "disappear" we usually mean it was on purpose. In our language we have words for it, gesgamugwa'latl and gesgamugwa'toq: you can make yourself disappear or somebody else can make you disappear. This man disappeared the winter before Geneviève and Paul Le Putois bashed in The Scotsman's head.

Although they were able to close their ears to it most of the time, any loggers that were working their way along Crête des Pins were bothered by the screams they kept hearing in the bush all the time. It must have bothered this one man a lot more because he ended up on The Scotsman's porch early one morning after The Scotsman had left to check his traplines. The man had waited half frozen in the bush until The Scotsman left because he had a pretty good inkling of what was going on and didn't want to stir things up worse.

Geneviève told the mother of One-Eyed Joe that when she first saw this man standing there she thought it was one of her spells—she was having a lot of them lately and she was afraid that the next time The Scotsman smacked her one, she wasn't going to wake up—but then she thought the man was maybe an angel. Then, since that sounded even crazier to her, she ended up saying "Allo?" and decided he was a real person when he said "Allo" back.

"Are you in some kinda trouble with your old man there?" he asked.

What was she going to say to him? Oh yeah, every day he pounds me until I piss myself so he can feel important. Her first concern as usual was not about herself, but to get this man to hell away as fast as she could do it. If The Scotsman returned while he was here, there was no telling what would happen. To her. To him. She was pretty much near the end of her ability to bother trying to withstand his abuse anymore, so now she just took it, her main concern being her five-year-old son who had to stand there and watch his father knock his mother out almost every day. He wasn't touching the boy yet, but she figured when her husband finally ran out of her, he was going to need somebody. And now she had to take on responsibility for this man who was standing on her porch thinking things could be as simple as walking away?

"Never mind me," she said. "But could you take my son?"

"Madame. Please. I hear you screaming every single night and I can't stand to listen no more. It's driving me out of my mind. It's bothering the other men, too. We can all hear you, you know. We're working Crête des Pins and the echo there is real loud and clear."

Geneviève was stunned. "Oh. You are the ones." She could feel the color draining out of her face and neck, her knees nearly buckling. She whispered: "My husband is listening to you talking right now! He was heading that way to check his traplines! That echo. That echo! You think I know nothing of that echo? You must go! And please. You must take my son with you." She snatched a jacket and two scarves off a peg that had been driven into the outside wall of the cabin. "I'll go inside, get him socks. A heavy shirt. Mitts, too. What else? It's going to be cold tonight. Please. Give me a short time to prepare something to take along for him to eat."

"But Madame—"

"With this back of mine... You see... I can't travel fast. Go now! Take him! Get him and yourself as far away from here as you can. But please. I ask only one thing: Get him to Port Royal and ask for the mother of One-Eyed Joe. She'll make certain the boy is well cared for."

"I can't leave you behind, Madame. It's unthinkable. What will he do to you if he comes home and finds his son missing?"

"Nothing he hasn't done before, I can assure you. And if he does? It will be a blessing. I can assure you of that as well. I'll just tell him the boy ran away."

"Madame. The prints of my snowshoes are much deeper than your boy's will be. It's obvious to anyone that a man has been here. Come with me now and we'll have time to get to the logging camp before dark. I know his kind. Your husband won't dare to take on all of us. You'll be safe with me."

Geneviève watched them until the last bit of the horizontal red stripe on her boy's jacket disappeared among the trees just over the rise. Her son had turned to look at her once but she waved him on, smiling as best she could with her misshapen face and her broken heart.

At least he's safe now, she whispered to herself.

She knew something had happened when her husband didn't return that night. He always came back the same day. If he was going to be longer, he would bring her and the boy along with him. When they went to the nearest settlement, which was twenty miles away, to get supplies each month—an arduous and painful trek for her—he needed her to haul the skid with his liquor while he carried the flour on his shoulder.

And during a good part of the homeward journey he would complain, loudest after she would cry out in agony when the skid dropped over a bump: "What's wrong with you now? I'm going to have to get myself an Indian wife. They know how to work. When you're all dried up down there and no more good, that's what I'm going to do. Get myself an Indian wife."

She knew that her husband and the kind logger had to have met up. Was it a sin, she wondered, to hope and pray that some stranger—an Angel—had come to earth to kill your husband? It probably was but she didn't care anymore, she prayed for it anyway.

She hadn't been able to sleep all night for listening behind the wind for the creaking of cold leather snowshoes, so by the morning she was exhausted. A strong wind had come up anyway so there was no way she could have heard him. He was just there. Their son with his eyes like an owl's eyes beside him. And a travois behind him full of meat.

"Woman. Cut this up proper and make us a meal. Store the rest."

Six

The Father called me into his yard one day as I was running past on the new snowshoes I'd just finished making for myself. I was proud of them. Even though I had to make them in a hurry because of the really early winter that year, they turned out better than I had ever done snowshoes before so when he first called me in, I thought he might have wanted to take a look at them. But I don't think he even noticed them. Maybe that was because it was early for people to be wearing snowshoes yet, leaves still hung onto their branches on the trees even though the snow was deep already. The Father was not like our people at all, our people noticed everything.

He waved me back behind his house where the whole yard had been emptied of snow. It had been cleaned so close to the ground even Orignal-Sale wouldn't make a footprint. Whoever had cleared the snow—and I'm sure it must have been Geneviève and it must have taken her most of the day so she was probably back at her wikuom sleeping by now—had had the good sense to pack it high against the outside walls of both the Father's house and the church. She had made white mountains all around the outside of his compound with the rest of the snow. You could sit there in the Father's back yard and feel like you were inside a cozy paper-birch basket.

I hadn't seen the shadowy ghostliness of Paul Le Putois for several days but that didn't mean he wasn't around; I could feel his owl's-eyes trying to penetrate my thoughts whenever I was anywhere near the church lately. I had mentioned this to the mother of One-Eyed Joe a few days earlier and she said: "He's curious. That's all. His father was Protestant. Probably filled his head with stories about Catholics. He's just trying to find out for himself. Still…" She laughed. "I wouldn't go into the bush with him just the same." She made a move to tickle my sides, trying to make a joke but it didn't work. He was starting to make me feel really uncomfortable. I was now starting to wonder if he knew I knew he was there. If maybe he thought I walked past the church on purpose to let him stare at me. With unhappy men like that you certainly didn't want to give them any encouragement, they dreamed up enough of their own in their own strange heads. Second Son used to stare at all our women exactly the same way with that pleading childlike sadness not just in the eyes but in the whole body. I don't think I could ever, ever feel that sorry for someone…

Like I said, I was more or less minding my own business trying out my new snowshoes that afternoon (trying to keep the thoughts of Paul Le Putois out of my head as much as possible as I passed the church), when the Father called out: "Marie-Thérèse, my child. I wanted to discuss a matter with you."

First of all… I hate that name. Second of all, I wasn't his child. Third of all, as I got closer to him, I saw that he had dragged two of his reed chairs close up behind his house and was pointing at one for me to sit in, which I did. Didn't he want anyone to see him talking to me? What was that all about? And fourth of all, I didn't want this man talking to me about anything after he had used his powers to enchant Feather against her own people. (It's easy to run stuff like that through your head as if you were really going to say something. But if you were afraid of somebody's bad medicine, you had to keep your mouth and your mind shut and not let them know.) And that thought added a fifth of all: Obviously he now had me believing that his medicine was stronger than the medicine of my own people. Maybe it was. But before I could open my tobacco pouch to sprinkle some around me, the Father interrupted my concentration with:

"You are seeing too much of Monsieur Guédry," he said. "Much too much. Stay seated, child! Hear me out!"

I mumbled something about not having seen "Monsieur Guédry" for half a moon, but I sat back down on the rickety reed chair anyway, fearful of toppling over onto the uneven ground back there behind his house. With my heavy parka on, I certainly wouldn't have hurt myself if I fell off his chair but dressed like I was, I barely fit in it. If I fell over, I'd more than likely break his prized chair. These chairs, five of them, had arrived early in the summer from the south—the White people called that land The Colonies—and the Father had been beside himself with excitement getting furniture made by White colonists even though they were Protestant and English. I believe it was the first and last time I ever saw him smiling. He had spent nearly a moon moving them around his yard until he finally settled on a section under some willows on the far side of the house from his church. He spent every afternoon out there—unless the weather was severe—and he would watch people go by and call some of them in off the path for tea. I suppose being a Father meant a lonely life.

"Don't you have Matins to say or something?" I asked him.

"Matins are said in the morning. Do you take nothing seriously, my child? Do you know nothing of the lust that wife-less ungodly men hold in their hearts toward young women? To marry early is a blessing from God almighty and you, my child, should be married as soon as possible. You are of age now. It's time for you to marry one of your own kind and start a family. Leave this godless Monsieur Guédry to his own devices."

I closed my eyes so the Father couldn't see me rolling them but I guess he thought I was having an attack of some kind because I heard his frozen chair squeak when he took his weight off it and I could feel and smell that he had stepped close to me. I opened my eyes again to see the purple and black material of his right sleeve flapping in front of me while he made that sign of his over my head.

"Well if that's all…" I said, starting to rise out of my chair. "I might as well be going now, e'e?"

He put his hand on the top of my head then and applied enough gentle pressure that I couldn't rise. "Stay seated, my child. We need to talk."

So he talked. And he talked. He talked for so long that he insisted on sending one of his lanterns with me, telling me I needed it to see my way home in the dark, telling me it was coming up to fall so the nights came more quickly every day—as if I didn't know this. I didn't need it but I didn't feel like arguing with him so I agreed and took the lantern from him.

"Good night, my child," he said to me as I was leaving. He was waving. I couldn't see him waving because my back was to him but I could hear it in his voice. "You can drop that off on your way back tomorrow."

Tomorrow? On my way back? I'd had enough of the Father to last me well into old age. I wasn't going back tomorrow. I would get one of our young ones to drop the lantern off. I thought Gi'gwesu, Muskrat, my little brother, would want to try out my snowshoes anyway, so I would offer him the chance.

At least I got to hear the story of Claude and Madame Louise, though. That made my time with the Father almost worthwhile. In fact, I was surprised at just how much the Father knew about it. I was thinking maybe Claude told him in Confession, but priests are never, ever to tell stuff you tell them in Confession, so I didn't know just how the Father could have known. I was also surprised that he seemed to have a great need to get the story of Claude and Madame off his chest. I think I just happened to be the one sitting there when he opened up that part of his memory where the story had been hidden away; and he told the story mostly like he was an ordinary man and not a priest, and like he was telling it to ordinary men and not to a young unmarried Mi'gmaw girl. Even though I'd heard some of it from Claude, I had learned a good lesson at the feet of the mother of One-Eyed Joe about keeping my mouth shut when someone is telling a story. I tried hard not to interrupt him. I had to bite my tongue more than once. And more than once, biting my tongue didn't work.

This is almost everything he said to me and the way he said it. I didn't know the meaning of every word he used, but my memory for words was always good:

There was a young woman—vraiment, une fille. Véronique. The young man's name was Guillaume but everyone called him Guy. He hated the name Guillaume. He thought it pretentious. Pretentious? It means affected. Affected! Hein? Hé bien alors! Tu comprends artificial?

Although they were young—she fourteen, he thirteen—it was not unusual that they be promised to each other in marriage so this was tentatively planned. It is the way things are done. Early marriage prevents a vast number of sins. They had known each other for only a few months and already Guy knew there would never be anyone else on this earth for him.

Her hair was the color of trembling aspen in autumn; her bones fine like those of the finch; her eyes like…

The young man's mother was Anne-Marie, the widowed sister-in-law of the Duchess of Calais, so the son was a bit of a catch by the circumstance of marriage, but unfortunately not by the circumstance of his family's finances. Anne-Marie was broke. Her late husband had squandered nearly everything they owned on whores and gambling. It was only by the uh… kindness of one of his many créditeurs that Anne-Marie was able to hold onto their home and its furnishings.

Yes, my child. This man also provided for her in other ways as well. Food. Servants. Clothing. Yes. Yes. Very kind of him.

The Father said this fast. It was like he was hoping I already knew what he didn't want to put into words.

No. There was no talk of marriage between them. He… He merely felt obliged toward her well-being. That's all. S'il vous plaît, Marie-Thérèse! Je veux continuer!

That's quite all right, my child.

Guy had attended many Friday evenings at the estate of the Marquis de Savoie. Anne-Marie and Louise, the wife of the Marquis, were friends but they were more friends of convenience than friends of the heart. What's that? Of course, they liked each other. They didn't know each other very well. That became quite apparent within the next two years.

Although being invited to the intimate Friday suppers with the Marquis and his wife was a regular event for his mother, this would be the first time that Guy, who had just turned thirteen, would be supping with the main party rather than taking his meal in the salon off the kitchen. It was quite a momentous occasion for him as he would be seated beside his beloved Véronique during supper. He would try his best to impress her, as well as her uncle, the Marquis. What a catch she would make! From all accounts, her dowry should be more than substantial.

This evening's meal was not only a special event for Guy, but for others as well. In some manner, it was in celebration of Guy's coming of age and his consequent eligibility for betrothal, but it was in large part a bon voyage party for the Marquis.

The Marquis—Philibert—would be off with an explorer he was financially backing to les Îles Galápagos within the week and there was his wife, Madame Louise, already entertaining her next lover at his table, under his—I would hope—unsuspecting nose, even while Philibert's side of the bed was still warm. Bien que, I must give Claude the benefit of the doubt as I believe that no one but Madame Louise knew of the trap that was being laid for him. Although Guy—aware of the fervor that beat within his own heart—was not unaware of the aura emanating from Madame to Claude. She had already had his older brother a few years previously. Anne-Marie, of course, was most certainly not aware of this side of her lady friend. At that time, neither lady knew of the other's petites manies.

The supper went well but young Guy began to notice that besides his hostess Madame Louise, his own mother was hanging onto Claude Guédry's every word. And to his great distress, his chère Véronique was much more interested in Claude Guédry than she was in Guy—What's that you say? Non? I was certain you said something. Hé bien.

Young Guy, of course, was heartbroken at this turn of events so he promised himself that he would never allow ce damné Claude Guédry to come between his love and himself if it was the last thing he ever did. Young love, hein? You must understand some of these feelings, Marie-Thérèse, do you not? Non?

Although Guy felt he was not as handsome as his new enemy in love, he was certainly charming, so it was très facile for him to convince Madame Louise to invite himself and his mother to stay as guests in the home of their soon-to-be-absent host. I believe that Madame Louise was simultaneously joyful and discontented with the arrangement but she kept these sentiments well hidden when her husband thundered:

"Magnifique! Quelle idée merveilleuse, mon garçon! My Louise would welcome the company of your mother while I'm away on my adventurous voyage to les Îles Galápagos. And you and my lovely niece will have a splendid chance to get to know each other. Hein?" He wiggled his eyebrows.

As it turned out, the young man's mother stayed only a few days, but the young man remained there for some time and was given his own room two doors down from Madame Louise. Hein? Ah, I believe the mother had uh… commitments at home.

My child. Were you married, you would not be risking your soul thinking along those lines! Now I want you to heed these words: Now these are not my words but the word of Notre Seigneur Jésus-Christ and that of his beloved ever-virgin mother Mary. You must marry. And you must stop seeing Claude Guédry. It's disgraceful what you two have been doing together! Do not look at me in that manner, Marie-Thérèse! It is disrespectful.

I accept your apology, my child. Although I do wonder about its sincerity.

Alors. After Philibert left on his voyage, Claude became a more and more frequent visiteur, and as the months passed into a year he had his own room at the estate of Philibert de Villegaignon, Marquis de Savoie.

Except during daily suppers, there was not much contact between Guy and Claude. I believe that Claude scarcely noticed the presence of Guy, often ignoring his comments at table and nearly every time upon passing him in the corridors of the château, he would simply not see him.

Guy had softened his stance on Claude since moving to Philibert's home to spend time with Véronique. Seeing that Claude spent most of his time in the company of Madame Louise helped, however his chère Véronique was still much too enamored of Monsieur Claude Guédry for Guy to feel entirely comfortable.

It was coming up to nearly two years that the Marquis had been away and there had been no reports of anyone seeing the *Ste-Cécile* nor her sister ships after they had passed Cape Horn going west nearly twenty-one months earlier. About four months after the Marquis's fleet left port, of two ships returning from their own trips past the area of the Galápagos

Islands, one reported that the *Ste-Cécile* had gone down at the Horn, and the other reported having seen her anchored off one of the Galápagos Islands. So much for the accuracy of news reported by seamen, hein?

Madame Louise appeared disheartened but never seemed distraught at hearing no news of her husband's whereabouts. I'm sure she must have been concerned in some manner. After all, his death would make her a very wealthy woman despite the inheritance laws governing those lost at sea. Most of the time she merely seemed preoccupied with Claude and their affair. Around this time, also, the gossip among the chateau's household was that Madame was with child.

Although the Kings of France tended to have illegitimate children on a regular basis, society tended to titter behind their fans about it and the children almost always had bright futures ahead of them. But any other child that was born on the wrong side of the altar could look forward to a life of little privilege and much scorn. France was, after all, a Catholic country. Although the child—if there were, in fact, a child—would be legally the child of her husband, once her husband was deceased she would no longer be married to him so the child would be illegitimate.

From the gossip that circulated later about the memorial banquet, it appeared to almost everyone who knew Philibert that Madame Louise was a little too anxious to hold the memorial which would signal her acceptance of the end of his life. Those close to her, of course, were compassionate about her need for haste and were quite aware that she had spent many hours, nay days, in deep contemplation regarding how she should handle her pregnancy. If someone came back with any proof at all that her husband had been dead for any length of time, the child would become illegitimate in retrospect. Her best course of action, then, would be to declare him dead and marry quickly before it became so obvious that she was carrying a child.

The memorial banquet was a grand one with every friend of the

Marquis she could remember to invite in attendance. She introduced Claude as her secretary: "Now that my dear, sweet husband is gone, there are so many, many matters to be dealt with. In my state of profound sorrow, I cannot handle these matters on my own. This young man has kindly accepted my offer of employment."

Most attendees were gracious enough to wait until they had gone home and were no longer under the roof of their hostess to make their disparaging comments, but others thought nothing of stating their opinions even at the supper table.

"Secretary? Watch when their eyes meet. You see that?"

"Since when does one's secretary sit at the head of the table?"

"I overheard two of my grooms talking last week. One is married to a servant of Philibert. They said his wife is pregnant! How amusing. Since the French Church no longer takes all her orders from the Vatican, does this mean that France now has its own Virgin Mary? Ha ha."

"I always knew she was a whore."

One of the older women: "I cannot say I blame Louise. I don't think it's a codpiece, do you?" The women near her laugh.

Madame Louise was not oblivious to their comments but acted as though everyone was having a marvelous time at the first large gathering she had put on alone without her husband and his connections. There were speeches, toasts, and eulogies to Philibert de Villegaignon, Marquis de Savoie, but when one rather unsavory-looking and very drunken man rose to toast The Assassin of King Wong, and was forcibly removed from the room, Madame was visibly shaken. The memorial banquet came to a close very shortly after that incident.

The man should not have been invited. His name was on a list of Philibert's acquaintances, which list she had found in the bottom drawer of the desk in his downstairs office. As soon as he arrived, Madame Louise knew exactly who he was but it seemed that she had never been aware of his real name. She had only known him by the name Monsieur Hébert.

What was it about Monsieur Hébert that had so frightened Madame?

Ah. One can never escape one's past.

Monsieur Hébert was one of the very few men in Saint-Malo who knew how Philibert had made his money.

Guy's apartments were only two doors from Madame Louise's bedroom so he was the first to reach her door when he heard her screams. Upon entering the room he saw Claude lying on the floor in a widening puddle of blood from a head wound. Monsieur Hébert was on top of Madame on the bed, and although she was stark naked it appeared that he was only trying to subdue her and not force himself upon her.

She screamed and scratched and kicked and bit but Monsieur Hébert continued to try holding her down. "Stop it, whore! Listen to me!"

Guy was young but his father had done one good thing for him: He had trained him how to fight with the sword. Guy glanced quickly around the room and spotted Claude's sword lying on a table. He grabbed it and cried out:

"Hé! Toi! You on the bed! Leave the woman be. Get off her now!" He pricked the side of the man's chest with the point of his sword.

Hébert rose rubbing his side, looking shocked at first. Then he began to laugh. He feinted left then right and snatched the boy's sword from his hand and hit him a glancing blow to the temple with the hilt. The boy crumpled.

When Guy's senses returned he heard the voice of Madame and the voice of Hébert in whispered but heated argument:

"I can pay you nothing until the lawyers agree that Philibert is dead."

"Sell your jewelry! You have enough of it. ha! Mon dieu! Why not sell yourself, whore? You used to make good money doing that."

Guy heard a grunt from Hébert and a whimper from Louise. From where he lay, he could at first see only the ankles and feet at the end of Hébert's legs that were hanging off the bed but if he turned his head, just so, he could see that Madame was lying there, a sheet tucked under her chin, her wrist enclosed in the intruder's huge hand. She twisted her arm and he let her go. She rubbed it, muttering.

Guy heard a clanking outside in the corridor and obviously the intruder heard it too.

"I must leave you now, Louise. It appears that proper enforcements have arrived." Guy heard the ropes of the bed creak as Hébert's weight came off it. He watched the man's shoes as they crossed the carpet toward the balcony where he must have gained entrance. He heard him speak.

"Think about it, Louise. Think about all that you have to lose."

Then everything disappeared for Guy once again.

If Madame Louise paid Monsieur Hébert any money, Guy was never a witness to the transactions, but he was quite certain that she must have. His own mother began showing up at their regular Friday evening suppers sporting jewelry that had once graced the throat, wrists, or fingers of Madame Louise. Occasionally, if he were on his balcony and the doors to Madame's chambers were open, he would be able to overhear conversations between the two women that proved it. He would often invite Véronique to listen as well. It was an exciting way of entertaining his beloved. Guy had heard that palace intrigue was an aphrodisiac.

They listened:

"You must tell Claude!" said Anne-Marie.

"I cannot. He would kill the bastard."

"Would that not solve your problem then? Are you a fool? Tell him!"

"I need Hébert alive, Anne-Marie. What he extorts from me is only a small price for what I gain from my association with him."

"You are going to have to give me more information, my friend. That is, if you wish to continue getting any sympathy from me. And that includes any further sales for your jewelry to my Stéphan. Come on! Tell me! What is your deep, dark secret? You can trust me with it."

"Very well. But you must promise me never to breathe a word of it to anyone on earth!"

"Done. And here's a kiss to seal it."

Seven

Most of what Father Soucy told me about Claude and Madame Louise was the same as what Claude told me about himself and Madame Louise except Claude hardly mentioned the boy Guy at all. I don't think Claude even knew the boy's name. Father Soucy was right about that, at least. Some of his story sounded strange to me for a couple of reasons: first of all, he made Claude out to be a bad person and I knew Claude well enough to say that the Father was wrong about that; and second of all, if everything he said was true, then Frenchmen were a lot stranger than I thought!

It seemed to me that I had the good luck to be able to watch two sides of the same story—well, three if you count Guy's and the Father's story as two. Sometimes the teller of someone else's story will turn it into an extra story. The French word for this is potins and our word for it is lutmaqan. It means to spread stories around as if they were true whether they're true or not. This was something the Grandfathers and Grandmothers told me I must never ever do as a Storyteller. But I think the Father might have done that because he didn't seem to like Claude Guidry at all. I didn't know why then but in time I found out.

Madame Louise ended up having Claude's baby boy but they didn't get to enjoy it very long because her husband, Philibert, showed up out of nowhere one day. He didn't exactly show up at the chateau "just like that," he got into port first and with all the excitement that he wasn't as dead as Madame had hoped he was, he wasn't able to get away from the port for almost two days. It was Monsieur Hébert who showed up "just like that" to ask Madame Louise for what the Father called an amazing amount of livres or else he'd tell the Marquis about her and Claude.

Of course Claude knew absolutely nothing of what Monsieur Hébert had been doing to her. Who was going to tell him? Madame? She had explained away Hébert's attack on them in her chambers by telling Claude the man was a lucky thief who'd gotten past the guards to steal her jewelry. One thing Madame was not was dull-witted. That's how she explained her missing jewelry. If Claude had found out the truth about her, he would have turned against her "just like that."

Véronique, who was now seventeen years old and still refusing Guy's hand in marriage, and who would forever refuse it, was the one who told Claude that he should grab all his important stuff and get out of the chateau, out of the city, and maybe even out of the country as fast as he could run. Claude told me he had never been more shocked in his life when the young woman came rapping at his door with information that would curl the hair of most men.

"Where did you get this information!" he demanded.

"Guy always knows when Monsieur Hébert arrives in Madame's chambers and he has promised to come fetch me each and every time so we can listen from Guy's balcony. Madame is not what you think she is mon cher Claude. She is evil."

"How could I not have known this about her? I have been under the same roof with this woman for nearly three years!"

"Mon cher Claude! Please tell me you are not that naive. You must have known something was amiss when her jewelry kept disappearing. Even the bracelet you yourself gave her is gone."

"It was stolen."

"It was not stolen. It was sold to the lover of Guy's maman for the money. Have you not seen Guy's maman wearing it? But no. Of course not. You have been completely blinded by your affections for Madame. You are thinking with your pénis, mon cher Claude. I had thought more highly of you." At this she tossed a purse onto Claude's bed telling him there was enough money in it to get him to Saint-Malo and passage on an outgoing ship. "If your brothers are still speaking to you after your shameful conduct here with the wife of Philibert de Villegaignon, Marquis de Savoie, perhaps they will allow you free passage on one of their slavers to the New World."

She turned back on the way out of Claude's room to add: "I would say to you, mon cher Claude: Do not go anywhere else but the docks. I fear that mon oncle Philibert might already know of your affair with Madame and he will surely kill both of you."

Claude took both her advice and her purse and left immediately. He knew if he went to see Madame Louise before leaving, he would not have been able to resist doing her harm.

I asked Claude what Madame Louise had done that was so horrible, but at first he wouldn't tell me any more about it than it had to do with getting young women from prominent families taken and selling them to people with what he called "strange tastes." I already knew about people who liked to steal women to lay with them—the mother of One-Eyed Joe had warned me about men like that (Jean-Baptiste Bourque had been one of them)—so I didn't see why that would make Claude suddenly turn to hating Madame so strongly for it. Like I told you before, some of us took wives from other Nations but never to hurt anyone.

I asked Claude again and I could see he did not want to tell me but I guess he knew I would never stop pestering him until he did, so he said there were some people who got excited only by killing women while they were penetrating them. And this was how Madame and her husband, Philibert, could afford to rival the King's suppers.

Once again I have to tell you that if I didn't know Claude Guidry as well as I did, I would never have believed him. But I did and I do. I never asked him any more about it.

It was the Father who told me what happened to Madame Louise and to Guy and Véronique when Philibert returned to his manor. And to this day, I still wish I had never gone back to the Father's to find out more about what happened to everybody. But we all make mistakes in our lives and some of us make bigger mistakes than other people do. My mistake was not trusting my instincts when I saw that look in the Father's eyes.

Eight

There was a bit of excitement went on in the village around this time. Actually, the excitement went on in the fort because everybody in the village was expecting something like it to happen for years so nobody was surprised.

Do you remember me telling you about Second Son of the Lnu Saqamaw? Well Second Son was older now but he hadn't got any smarter. All that time of drinking brandy and beer and wine had made his brain rot, so although he forgot things most of the time, he also remembered things sometimes. This time he forgot to keep his mouth shut if he saw Paul Le Putois around, but he remembered—after all these years—that Paul Le Putois had been the one who shot Jean-Baptiste Bourque in the back that time out at Mouse Ridge when he had forced himself on Young Rabbit Woman. So Second Son sees Paul Le Putois hiding behind the church and off he goes running to the fort to alert the soldiers about it.

I know he didn't do it out of meanness. He did it so his wife—yes, he finally got one!—would think he was a shaman and start doing what she was told. He didn't tell her that he had seen the real Paul Le Putois behind the woodshed near the Father's church (which was the truth). He told her he had seen Le Putois in a vision. To be honest with you, I would have believed him about the visions myself, but never the shaman part. They say he used to have visions all the time when he was using the liquor, but having those kinds of visions doesn't make you a shaman no matter how much you wanted to be one.

His father wasn't the Lnu Saqamaw, the chief, anymore and hadn't been for a while, so the parents of his wife, Apalqaqamej, Chipmunk, didn't give her away trying to be better than other people, they gave her away because they wanted to get their daughter married off and they didn't care who to. When she was little, a moose knocked her over—and this was why I named Claude's first pig l'Orignal Sale—and she hit the front of her head on a rock. This injury didn't make her stupid. She was very able to do everything a wife needs to do for her husband and children, but it made her say out loud, no matter who was around, every single thing she thought about. So everybody hated her. Second Son must have hated her too, sometimes, because she told a lot of secrets about him to anyone who would listen. Some of the women would even ask her right out what it was like laying with Second Son, and she would tell them everything and complain about it. We got a lot of laughs that way.

The soldiers at the fort had never heard of Jean-Baptists Bourque so they didn't care if somebody shot him ten summers ago. A lot of the newer soldiers looked down their noses at the coureurs de bois anyway, saying they were nothing but outlaws because they kept selling their own furs despite being told that they had to go through the Ministère de la Marine if they wanted to continue dealing in the furs they trapped or traded with The People for. It was the Law, the soldiers said. The coureurs de bois would tell the soldiers that the Law didn't apply to them because they lived in l'Acadie, not in the settlement at Québec, so they were going to keep on doing what they'd been doing for all those winters they'd been doing it, and the soldiers couldn't stop them. One of the chiefs at the fort told us that the truth was, the soldiers didn't want to hear anything about the coureurs de bois that would give them any more work than they already had because it wasn't any of their business in the first place. "We have enough of the coureurs de bois in the today without having to deal with them in the yesterday," the superior said. Anybody who had been at the fort when it happened, and remembered about the shooting of Jean-Baptiste Bourque, just turned their faces away from Second Son and tried to make out that he was making up stories again even though he knew and they knew he wasn't.

Feather's soldier told her he wanted to keep her safe so without asking for permission from his superior at the fort, he went out to the church with Second Son to look around for Paul Le Putois. By this time, though, somebody from our village had run over to warn Paul Le Putois that he'd better take off for a while in case they came looking for him. They covered up his tracks and he left.

Nine

Gi'gwesu, my little brother, told me he had better things to do than run errands for his sister and refused to bring the Father's lantern back, even if I gave him my new snowshoes as a gift. He said my snowshoes were so ugly he wouldn't use them if he was trapped in the bush in a blizzard cold enough to crack the hide of a bear. I had to go back to the Father's myself. By the time I got there it was snowing wet and heavy so the Father said I should come inside his house or I'd get sick.

"Come in. Come in," he said taking the lantern from me. I'd wrapped it in skins to keep the snow off it. "You're soaking wet. You'll become ill. Here. Sit by the fire. Give me your parka and I'll shake it off outside."

I'd never been in the Father's house since before my uncle and some of the other men in my village had helped him finish it, so I was interested in what it looked like from the inside with the glass in the window and the door on. Because I was tall, I thought the nicest part about White men's houses was that I didn't have to walk around the edges leaning over like I had to do in our wikuom. I thought I might like living in a house like this.

"It's nice in here," I said. "I didn't think it would be this warm. What did you call this big thing in the middle of the room?"

"C'est une cheminée, a fireplace. It's for heating and cooking."

"How do you make the stones stand on top of each other like that?" I'd seen these structures at the fort, but didn't know what you called them or how they were built. The first time I saw one, I thought it was a clumsy way to hold up what they called un plafond, a ceiling. The Father explained that the stones were stuck together with mortar, and mortar is made from quicklime, water and sand. Quicklime is from burning limestone a certain way and you can get that from The Colonies, which is what he did. I asked him why they didn't make it in Québec and he said they made it there but he preferred to get his stuff from The Colonies. He said the only things you can't get from The Colonies is stuff for the church.

"They're not Catholic," he said.

I already knew that.

I asked him about his dirt floor, too, and why he didn't cover it with evergreen branches like we did. He pointed to his chairs and his wooden bed and said he didn't need to because he had furniture and added quickly, like he was ashamed, that it would be nice to have a proper foundation dug in the earth with a proper wood floor built over it with beautiful rugs, and a second story up there to sleep and store things in, and with actual walls, but a priest is supposed to make certain sacrifices and unless or until he became Pope he would have to settle for the simple things in life.

I got the feeling then that the Father had already lived like the Pope at some time in his life and that this life of priesting was not something he liked at all. I asked him straight out about it, why he had become a Father if he didn't like it and all he did was look at me with the saddest smile on his face that I have ever seen.

"Love, Marie-Thérèse. Lost love is what reduced me to this life. This land. This godforsaken place. This— This hovel." And he began to cry. He put his face into his hands and sobbed like a woman.

I didn't know what to do so I stood up and put my arms around him, trying to comfort him, rocking him back and forth like you would a baby, when suddenly his arms went around me and he was kissing me all over my face and neck.

A lot of what happened after that I can only tell you what it looked like and not what it felt like because I suddenly wasn't there underneath him on the dirt floor anymore. I remember falling onto my back with the pressure of his weight on me and his hard knuckles digging into the inside of my upper legs when he forces them apart, and I remember being angry because my hair is getting full of dirt. After that I'm watching from up in the air.

I see a man in a black dress with purple trim on top of a Mi'gmaw woman whose eyes are as round as Paul Le Putois's eyes and the fear in them is the same fear as in Paul Le Putois's eyes when he was a child. The man in the dress pushes one of his forearms against the Mi'gmaw woman's throat and with his other arm he lifts his dress up and does something to the trousers he's wearing underneath. He pushes the Mi'gmaw woman's long shirt up and out of the way as he pries her legs open with his free arm and with both his own legs like you'd pry open the belly of a fish to take the guts out. The Mi'gmaw woman makes the strangest sound. The man moves his arm off her throat and puts his hand over her mouth. She is making that awful sound. I guess the man doesn't like it either. Then he lifts up her behind and thrusts himself against the private space between her legs and she screams against his hand. Even his hand can't stop that scream from coming out of her and piercing the walls of the cabin. The eyes of the Mi'gmaw woman become round flint stones and the man groans and slumps on top of her.

The next thing I am doing is lifting the flap away from the entrance to the Moon Time wikuom. It isn't time for my Moon Time but I am bleeding so I must have thought I should go to the Moon Time place. I hurt and it feels like my legs are coming out from a different place on my body. The thing I want to do most of all is melt snow to clean his slime and my blood off me. I don't like how I smell. I can smell his way of cooking off me. It rises off my clothes. Between my legs it is slippery and it stinks of something unfamiliar that I don't like. Some of the quillwork on my shirt is broken and crushed and that makes me sad but I can't cry. The front of my neck hurts. It is still hard to breathe. I have clean clothes in the Moon Time wikuom but the skins in the sleeping area are cold. At least there is wood. I don't think I could walk far to gather some especially on snowshoes which stretch me open. It hurts to walk. It hurts to breathe. It hurts to think. It hurts to feel. It hurts to be.

Ten

My head was starting to clear by the next morning and I noticed that outside the Moon Time wikuom there was a package. The only one I could think of who would have put it there was Paul Le Putois but I thought he was away in the bush again to keep the soldiers at the fort from finding him. It could only have been him.

When I opened the package I knew for sure it had to be Paul Le Putois who had left it because of what was inside. It was partridge meat prepared exactly the way his mother, Geneviève, made it for her son. She didn't make it for me. When you made something for Paul Le Putois, you had to make sure it looked exactly like the animal it came from or else he wouldn't eat it. Remember I told you he didn't like meat? That somebody else had to prepare it for him? While the partridge meat was cooked and it would have suited Paul Le Putois very well, it didn't look good to me because the feet were still on it, with the ankle feathers making it look like it was getting ready to go dancing at a powwow and not into my stomach. But I was really hungry so I ate it anyway after I twisted the feet off.

Men did not come near the women's Moon Time wikuom but Paul Le Putois was never one to do as he was told. It certainly wouldn't have been one of the other men from the village. It wouldn't have been one of the women either because almost all of us had been here half a moon ago. We always seemed to get our Moon Times at the same time.

I wondered how much Paul Le Putois knew about what had happened at the Father's. If he was away hiding in the bush how did he know what went on? I know I didn't scream a lot—maybe just the once—because the Father had his elbow on my throat crushing it most of the time. I could barely breathe, how could I scream? Paul Le Putois had no Mi'gmaw blood in him but he was able to know things the same way we knew things: we just knew them.

The bleeding had stopped but I was still sore and my upper legs ached like crazy so I didn't feel like walking all that distance home on my snowshoes. The other thing was that I didn't want anybody in the village to know what had happened. I knew they would know just from looking at my face that I was different. I couldn't stay at my Moon Time wikuom for much longer, though, because they would be suspicious when I came here again when my real Moon Time was due. Three times in one moon would make people think I was sick.

Instead, I collected firewood and piled it in the wikuom and then I replaced all the branches on the floor and hung the bedding skins and furs outside to freshen. When I was doing this, I heard the soft sound of snow being stepped on but when I turned toward the sound, there was nothing there. I knew then for sure that Paul Le Putois had not run away into the bush, he was still close by.

"Thank you for the food." My words slid past the trees and over the high snow drifts. I know he heard me because I could feel him listening.

☽ ○ ☾

My next Moon Time didn't come so I knew the worst had happened. I was with child. Among my people this meant you were now married to the man you had lain with but I did not wish to be married to the Father even if he could be married to me. The older people would be wondering who the father of my baby was and there was no way I was going to tell them what really happened. For one thing, I was ashamed of what had happened to me for teasing him when I was young and used to sit in the front row at Mass to make his face go red.

Somewhere inside me a voice was telling me that the Father had done it to hurt Claude Guidry in some way because Claude and I were such good friends. I think the Father was surprised to discover that I bled when he lay with me. I think he expected I had been laying with Claude Guidry all this time. I knew different, though. I had heard that Claude Guidry was laying with the widow of Martin Dugas whose body some of the runners had found frozen out in the bush last winter. Marguerite Petitpas had a young son and a baby on the way and no one to look after her.

Because Claude was my friend and we could tell each other anything, I decided I would tell him I was with child but I didn't want to have to tell him who the father of my baby was or how I got this way. I was sure he would kill the Father and that was about the only thing I had learned from the Father that I believed: killing a Father was a very bad thing. Among my people, if you killed what the White people called our "medicine man" you would have bad medicine on yourself and on your family for the rest of your life and the rest of your children's lives, too. I wasn't about to make Claude and his descendants suffer for all eternity for something that was my own fault.

☽ ○ ☾

Around this time, my friend Feather began to believe that her soldier from the fort was going to take her to the land of his King with him—on his King's ship! And with all the other soldiers returning home, too, and with her being the only female on board.

I told Feather she had been crazy getting involved with a soldier from the fort especially when their "Pamphlet"—their rules for soldiers—said he shouldn't be with her at all. She told me it was God's will that she should marry this man. Father Soucy said so, too, she said. So I told her what I thought of Father Soucy. As far as I was concerned he was his own devil that he was always telling us about. She didn't know that I was carrying Father Soucy's baby in my belly and I didn't tell her.

I had told no one that I had a baby in my belly because I had hoped to make it go away. But because of the early snows that year, the special plants I needed to use for that were covered up or gone to sleep for the winter. It was looking like the Father's medicine would make me have this baby even though I didn't want it. Every time I had my sickness in the mornings it made me think of that terrible night when the Father hurt me. I knew if I had this baby I would be thinking of that night until I died.

It was not only Feather who believed every word the Father told her. Many of our people were starting to trust him more than they trusted our Grandfathers and Grandmothers. The Father knew nothing of the ways of our people no matter how much we tried to teach him and he made us feel that we were always wrong about everything now. The ways of our ancestors had become bad. Even if he had not done the bad thing to me I would still not be able to look into his eyes without moving my face away from him. If you always feel bad whenever you're with someone, something is wrong.

I was thinking that Father Soucy's medicine made some of my people turn stupid. Many times I have seen my people ask the priests a question and they were told not to think that way or they would go to Hell. Who would ever want to make people turn their brain off from thinking? Kji Niskam, the Great Spirit, makes us think, makes my people think all the time. My people must figure things out by themselves, like working with quills or with beads or making our canoes better and faster, and using bark and bones to make more and more tools. Our mothers and fathers show us the materials that worked for them and sometimes we watch them work but they expect us on our own to learn new ways to do things and to help each other learn new ways, too. If nobody learned new ways we would never have learned to hunt, or build a canoe, or start a fire with sticks or flints in the first place. Our dreams show us what we must do so we put into practice what our dreams tell us. If what we try does not work then we must try again.

The soldiers came from a land called France which was where Claude's King lived and each group of soldiers would stay on our land at the fort for three summers and then would return to their King. Time was up for the soldier that Feather loved.

"I prayed that the snows would come early and they have," she told me, all happy, thinking that this should mean that she and her soldier would be staying for another winter because the ships wouldn't sail.

"You haven't heard, then." I didn't want to be the one to tell her but it looked like I was going to be the one anyway.

"Heard what?" Her hand went to her throat.

"They are getting ready to set sail with the tide tomorrow." I wondered if her soldier was being cruel or kind. "You didn't know? He didn't tell you?"

"He won't leave me behind. He loves me. He told me so. And he knows that Father Soucy insists that we marry."

"Ah. You are with child then." And I almost told her right then that I was, too.

Her mouth dropped open wide with anger and this made her look funny so I wanted to laugh but there was nothing funny about it. Not at all. I would be losing my friend forever if she married the soldier and went away with him.

"I am not."

I told her she would die if she went to see Claude's King. Our people always die when they go to see the King. The King's food and the King's land and the King's ways make them sick and they die. I began to feel very sad knowing that if my friend Feather went to see the King she would die and I would never see her again.

Feather told me she was not going to die in the land of the King. She said God would look after her because she believed in notre Seigneur Jésus-Christ. And if she did not marry she would go to Hell because she had impure thoughts and desires.

"Only thoughts and desires?" I asked her. "Not actions, too?"

"Of course not!" She turned her reddening face away from me.

I could always tell when she was lying so this time I laughed at her but she looked so hurt I stopped laughing and suggested that maybe her soldier could leave the fort and come live in our village with us. "Does he know how to hunt and trap?"

To this she said nothing but I could see that she was thinking and then she told me that her soldier (François d'Orléans was his name), did not know how to hunt or trap but he could shoot a target with his gun and he was accomplished with the sword and he was from a good family.

Ah. Bon élevage, I thought. Like Claude. Or maybe like the little red piglets of Orignal-Sale.

I told her to pray to her God and to get Father Soucy to pray to his God, too, that they never had any children or else they would all starve to death. You can't eat a sword.

I could not understand why she was so against being with one of our own people. There was a village only one day's journey from us and I heard that two of the young men there were looking to find wives for themselves. One of them had lost his own wife in childbirth before the snows came. I heard that this one was a kind man and very handsome to look at and that he was one of the best hunters in the village. The other was his very good friend and an equally good hunter. I asked her again why she did not want to marry one of our own people and she told me: "They're savages."

Now I understood.

Eleven

Feather took it a lot harder than I thought she would when her young man—excuse me, "her fiancé"— François d'Orléans went back to live in the land of his King without her. She took it so hard I didn't even remind her how many times I told her this was going to happen. I tried to be her friend even though she didn't want me to be her friend anymore. She didn't want any of us to be her friend anymore and she went away with one of the coureurs de bois. For our women, that was worse than killing yourself. Killing yourself was a quicker and easier way to die. A lot easier.

The Runners of the Woods had it in their heads that they were big shots because they got money and food and ammunition and supplies for the furs and the other stuff they took from the land and all the Mi'gmaq got was what was left and a lot of half-breed babies. But not all of the Runners treated their women like what comes out of a fish's gut if you nick it with your knife when you're cleaning it. Claude Guidry didn't. And Paul Le Putois, Paul the Skunk, was mixed up and sometimes as dangerous as a wolverine with the clenched-jaw illness, but he would never harm a woman. At least not on purpose. But things were getting more and more difficult for the Runners now that more Newcomers were arriving at the settlement at Québec and the Hudson's Bay Company was taking over more and more land where the Nēhiraw lived. The Nēhiraw were people that the French called Cri and they lived very far away. No one I knew had ever met one of the Nēhiraw but those from away said they were tall people with beautiful slanted eyes and darker skin that most of us had. Claude told me that the King of the maudits anglaises was ruining Claude's life because that King was making Claude's King act the same way, taking over great areas of the land and wanting to control everything and everybody with rules and obligations. "I am no one's indentured servant nor shall I ever be one," Claude said. "I won't be owned by anybody and if it comes to that, I will stop trapping and stick with raising pigs." None of the other runners was happy about the gradual changes, either. I think hearing these things made them drink more alcohol and cheat each other—and us—more often.

Around this time, a lot of other things happened, too. The first one was that the mother of One-Eyed Joe came up to me one day. She came up so quietly behind me that I jumped when she touched my shoulder.

She laughed. I didn't.

She told me my mother had come to her with a problem and the problem had to do with me. I knew right away what she meant because things had been smelling bad to me lately and I had told my mother two times that the pemmican we were about to eat smelled funny. Because my mother was known for her good pemmican, this was a surprise to her but my mother didn't get angry about that at all. Instead, the second time I said it, she made a joke. But she took the joke back right away because it might have been funny on the way out of her mouth but it wasn't funny when it went into her ears: "What's the matter? Did that Frenchman get you with child or—? Oh."

The next thing I know, the mother of One-Eyed Joe has startled me so badly I nearly jumped off my snowshoes.

"Come with me," is all she said and I followed her to her wikuom. When we got there, she told me to sit down and keep my mouth shut. Then she went into a long story about how bad it was to get mixed up with Frenchmen and especially the soldiers at the fort. "Just ask Hélène—"

I couldn't help myself. "Feather."

She gave me a look that made me turn my head away for fear that the arrow coming out of her eyes was real, then she continued. "Just ask Hélène about that. You'll find out from her that most of the coureurs de bois are not ones to get yourself involved with."

I was good and didn't tell the mother of One-Eyed Joe that I wasn't blind and deaf, just with child. But I did say, "I'll ask Feather about that, too."

She got up from the kaksk'ug then and motioned for me to do the same. "I'll speak to the Frenchman today," she said.

"His name is Claude and it isn't him. Please don't say anything to him. Please. It isn't him."

"Very well then. Now go. Go about your business."

And that was that. Or so I thought.

The next thing I knew, the whole village was all a-scurry preparing for a gathering. Everyone from the next village had been invited and there would also be races and dancing and singing ceremonies.

"Dancing and singing ceremonies and a gathering in Penamujuiku's month? It's the middle of winter," said Feather to me after she told me about it. "What are the Grandfathers and Grandmothers thinking?" She paused for a moment then we both rolled our eyes and laughed. She had come back to the village because a runner she had been with had gone away. It was the first time I'd heard her laugh in a long time. Maybe the coureurs de bois were good for her after all. "It's because of me, isn't it?" She looked up at me from the corner of one eye like she used to all the time before her heart got broken by the soldier from the fort. That made me feel good. "They want to get me married off and into another village before I disgrace myself any further with the runners."

I reassured her that she wasn't the only disgraced young woman around but didn't go into detail.

She looked at me out of the corner of her eye again with something between admiration and surprise. "So it's true then. The Frenchman got you."

"His name is Claude and no it wasn't him." I was beginning to echo like the hills in Île Royale and so was everybody else.

☽ ○ ☾

Feather's life with the coureurs de bois wasn't as bad as it was for many of our women and that was because of Paul Le Putois. Although the runners often traveled together for safety, they each had their own trapline and they checked their own traps regularly and skinned their own animals and some tanned their own hides. So on the traplines, they were more alone than not and this was also because those who had learned how to tan their own hides didn't want anybody learning how by watching them do it. They wanted to be alone for that. Except for women. They all wanted a woman along to share their sleeping furs with. If you dared to steal from another man's trap, you were as dead yourself as the animal you'd stolen. The only exception was if there was a rabbit in the trap and you had been injured or somehow needed the rabbit for food and there were no birch trees around to eat the bark of. The rabbit's skin, of course, would go to the owner of the trapline. And if you wanted to remain on good terms with the owner of that skin, you would prepare it first or pay one of our people to do it for you. But there were as many exceptions as there were men as far as their women went. Some of the men were like those in the North, willing to share, but most would kill you and the woman if they found you together. No exceptions there.

Most runners—and especially their women—disliked Paul Le Putois intensely but they tolerated his presence as we all did when he followed along behind and this might have been mostly because he didn't do it all the time. It would have been different if he was along watching everybody do everything they did every minute of the day. I heard stories that Paul Le Putois even watched men and women relieve themselves but I didn't believe these stories at all. I'm not sure if I didn't believe them because I just didn't or because I didn't want to think that he might be watching me sometimes doing private things. I know that some of the runners wanted him to follow along with them because he was an excellent tanner of hides and also because he could sneak up on the most wary of animals whether he was upwind or down. He was clean, too, and was very careful to pick out the last little bit of fur or flesh from the teeth of traps before washing them with hot water and drying them off before he re-set them. It saved a lot of work for the runners, they said. I heard a couple of the men laugh and say "If only he had breasts he would make a good fur companion." They said this to mean they thought he was womanly. I didn't at all think he was womanly, he was intent on small details and liked to make certain that everything was where and how it should be. Feather said he didn't smell the same as the other White men to animals because he didn't drink alcohol anymore and also bathed on a regular basis, melting and heating up snow in the winter and washing himself all over.

One of the reasons the runners didn't like Paul Le Putois going anywhere with them was because they had to prepare his meat for him (even though he provided his own and most of the time theirs, too) but it was mostly because they were afraid of him. If they got carried away when they were drinking—especially if they treated a woman badly (and this was why the women tolerated Paul Le Putois, but only so far)—they were in danger of becoming food for the scavengers.

I hadn't realized how hard the life of a coureur de bois was until

Feather told me some of the things she had seen while going with them onto the land. At first, she followed a man they called Lesui'p and explained that according to the Father, this man Lesui'p was the same race as Jesus was. There was supposed to be a big difference between a Lesui'p and a Frenchman but she said she didn't notice any difference at all. She liked him because he was very kind to her but the other men didn't "because of his race" he told her, so he went away and she came back to our village.

Twelve

Our village was busier than it had been for four moons. The men were clearing off spaces in the snow where the land underneath it was the flattest and the women were making the decorations or cooking stuff or searching through their wikuoms for special body decorations when Claude came up behind me. He didn't scare me like the mother of One-Eyed Joe had the day before because I knew him so well I could always sense when he was near.

He grabbed me by the elbow almost making me drop my end of the finish line rope that Feather and I were braiding out of kaksk'us bark for the races. "Come with me," he said. To say he was upset would be saying a waterfall and the drip of sap from a snawe'l were the same thing.

"What?" I asked him, pulling my arm away from him. "I have a lot of work to do before the guests arrive. We have only three days. If I don't do my share, the mother of One-Eyed Joe will scalp me."

At the other end of the braided rope, Feather gasped at me. "Oh! You are so disrespectful, Marie-Thérèse. We do not scalp people."

"That's not what I heard about us from some of the Newcomers." I meant her precious soldier and his friends and she knew that's who I meant. "I don't know where some of these Newcomers got their ideas from." And I gave her a look that made her turn her head away toward the little ones who were plucking the small brown cones for their tossing game off a tamarack tree at the edge of the clearing.

"Come here and hold this end of the finish rope, Atu'tuej," she said to one of the boys then turned back to me. "Go. Go talk with your husband." She said this so loudly several of the women around us laughed.

Apalqaqamej, the wife of Second Son, and whose baby was about to be born any day now, pointed at me. "The widow of Martin Dugas will be hunting you down, Keskoua. You better watch out! Marguerite Petitpas will skin you from your toes to your nose when she catches you. And in your condition, she will catch you real easy. She's not with child anymore and you are. You're getting fatter and she's skinny and strong again." And she started to laugh so hard she had to sit down on the pile of snow behind her.

Feather came over and snatched my end of the finish line rope from me and bumped my body away from hers. "Go. Go with your husband."

I went because Claude had grabbed my elbow again and was leading me out of the village toward another clearing, already emptied of snow, for some privacy near the high rock face that we called The Bear's Behind, but on the way I stumbled and the anger went out of his face right away as he reached with his other arm to steady me. "Mon Dieu, are you all right, Keskoua? Did you hurt yourself?"

"There's nothing wrong with me except that people don't know how to mind their own business. What's wrong with *you*?" I knew but I was trying to pretend I didn't now that I was getting a little bit of sympathy from him. I was going to go have a talk with the mother of One-Eyed Joe as soon as I could get away from Claude.

We reached the clearing where I was surprised to see that someone had already placed extra half-log seats around the fire circle in preparation for the gathering. The rocks for the fire were always in place but there was no wood in it yet. The Bear's Behind, green with wet lichens at this time of year, rose up above the pine trees. The Bear was a sacred place so at first I wondered why Claude had brought me here. Then I realized that he knew I would have to tell the truth in a sacred place. Especially with The Bear so close.

The Bear's Behind was part of The Bear, a huge upthrust of rock that the Grandfathers told us had bubbled up from deep down in the heart of Mother Earth before The People came; it had formed a long broad ridge that looked like a bear standing there. It even had a bulge at the front of it that some said looked like its head was looking back at something. I could never pick out the head as a head no matter which side I looked up at The Bear from, except that a clump of kaksk'ug on top of it did look like an ear if I closed one eye and squinted the other. One of its back legs, the one on the other side from me and Claude now, stuck farther out to the side than the others so if you were careful, you could climb up onto The Bear's back there. But nobody did. Or would. A long time ago somebody had started to chip out toe and finger holds but had stopped half way up that back leg so there were stories went around about why. But nobody knew for sure. One of the stories had to do with The Bear's head turning back to look, that maybe when you got up that high, the face of The Bear was easier to see, that maybe it wasn't happy about having little bugs like us on its leg. When we were little, Feather and I used to wonder about that. I think other people wondered about that, too, because nobody ever climbed up there. At least nobody who would talk about it if they did. When I went up to The Bear's back later on and only because I had to, I didn't want to talk about what I saw either, but not because I was afraid of The Bear. At least I don't think that was the reason. Sometimes we don't know the real deep-down reason we are afraid of things, or even if we are, and maybe that's good sometimes.

"Sit," Claude told me.

People were always telling me to sit lately. I was going to start getting annoyed about this sooner than later but for now, I did as I was told.

"You know what I'm going to say, don't you?" said Claude, shaking a finger in my face.

"Put that finger away. You know I hate it when you do that."

This made him shake it more for telling him not to shake it. "What is this business I hear that you are enceinte and I am supposed to be the proud papa and marry you? I haven't ever touched you. I wouldn't touch you if you were the last woman in l'Acadie. You're just a kid."

"And I wouldn't touch you if you were the last man." What else could I say?

He sat down beside me. "Écoutez. Écoutez bien, damoiselle." He put his finger away but I knew he still wanted to point it into my face because he laced his hands together and put them between his legs and closed his thighs around them. "Are you listening?"

"Yes, I'm listening. How could I not be listening? You're right in my face. If I was deaf I could still hear you. So can everybody else." I had just caught a glimpse of Paul Le Putois changing trees over by The Bear's Behind.

The finger almost escaped its bonds. "If I ever hear again that you are telling such stories about me, you will be in big trouble. I will no longer be your friend. Do you understand?"

"I didn't—"

"And furthermore," he said. "If you are hoping to get yourself a husband at the ceremonies tomorrow, you would be wise not to go around telling lies to everybody that you are with child."

"But I a—"

"And furthermore—"

"Stop it," I said. "Just stop it. I *am* with child. And I told no one—no one—that you are the father." I could feel my throat tightening up like it always does just before my eyes start to fill up with water so I tried to concentrate on slowing down my breathing but it was of no use. I was going to cry and it was going to be loud and long.

"What are you saying?" The look on Claude's face, with his jaw open like that and his eyes all big, were exactly what I needed to stop the flood of tears. I burst out laughing.

"There's nothing funny here, Keskoua. Are you really with child?"

I nodded, still with a smile on my face even though water was in my eyes for sure now.

"How can this be?" His face was now turning fatherly and serious and as full of love and concern as I had ever seen it. "We have no secrets between us. You would have told me if you had fallen in love with someone." He let his hands escape their trap of thighs so he could bring them to cross his arms over his chest. He leaned away from me. "You would have told me." A look of hurt passed over him but he did a good job of hiding that very quickly. "Wouldn't you?"

"I'm not telling anybody anything." I crossed my arms, too. "It's nobody's business."

"It's certainly my business if you're telling everybody I'm the papa."

"I didn't. Everybody just thinks that because we're friends. They need to mind their business. It's none of their business."

"It's somebody's business. It's the father's business. He is now your husband."

"NO HE IS NOT!" I screamed at Claude and got up and ran out from the clearing as Paul Le Putois's shirttail disappeared past The Bear's Behind. "NO! HE IS NOT! NEVER NEVER NEVER!"

As I ran by where they were working, the men and women and even all the young ones who were preparing for the gathering stopped what they were doing to look over at me with frowns on their faces.

Thirteen

Claude didn't speak to me for the next two days even though we were both almost side by side all the time while we worked on preparations for the gathering, but he kept looking over at me all the time—especially at my stomach—which made everybody else look at my stomach, too.

Early the morning of the third day, I was about to yell at him to stop when Gi'gwesu came running into the compound to say that our guests were at the final pathway, the spot where three paths there joined into one.

"They're coming. They're coming," my little brother said, all excited, cold-air clouds coming out of his mouth and floating away behind him. "And Falcon is with them!" He came sliding to a stop beside me and put on a stupid smile that was supposed to tell me some secret family thing between him and me but I pretended not to notice. I knew he had been listening when our mother and the mother of One-Eyed Joe had been trying to figure out the best man to set me up with and Falcon's name had come up. Trouble is, Feather noticed me pretend not to notice and the corners of her mouth turned way down. Since she had returned to the village her moods jumped up and down like a chickadee in flight.

Ah, I thought. *Feather doesn't think Falcon is a savage, though, does she?*

She must have been able to see what I was thinking because her face went red and she turned away.

Gi'gwesu noticed this from Feather, too, and he made a slight movement of his head toward her and whispered, "Don't worry, Keskoua, you can out-dance Feather any day. He won't even see her."

His face told me that he was expecting that I would be happy with what he was saying but I was still holding in my anger at Claude and at everybody else, too, and I let it out at Gi'gwesu. "Mind your own business." My moods were flying around, too.

Hurt flew across his face like a bat across the moon at dusk and I felt bad right away for snarling at him but he returned my words with another whisper. "I know you love Claude the Woodsman but Falcon is a good hunter. He is almost the best in their village." He glanced down at my stomach. "You can hardly tell anything yet, big sister. Just wear a loose dress. Hunch over like Paul's mother, Geneviève, does. No one will know."

I was about to tell him it was too late, that everybody already knew, when a big commotion at the far end of the village stopped me.

Falcon had arrived and he was dressed in the most beautiful parka I had ever seen. I knew somehow that his wife, who was from the North and who had died having his baby at the end of summer, had made it for him. His hair was unbraided, the mark of a single man and there was one eagle feather tied into it at the side of his head. Beside him stood his friend, Sleeping Cougar. All the children from our village—boys and girls alike—crowded around Falcon as if there was no one else standing there and not fourteen or fifteen other people. The little ones chattered away at him like red squirrels fighting.

"Will you be running in the three-legged race?"

"Did you bring your special bow?"

"Can I be your partner?"

"I heard your arrows are the straightest of anyone's."

"Will you be in the target competition?"

"I made four targets all by myself."

"How did you bring back the moose alone that time?"

"You will see them."

"My targets look like grouse."

"He made a toboggan, don't you know anything?"

"Mine look like turkeys."

"I know he made a toboggan."

"You must be very strong to pull a whole moose along when there's no snow."

"Of course he's strong, look at him."

Giggles and smiles and much jabber filled the edge of the clearing near the tamarack tree.

Falcon looked out at the rest of us over the heads of the little ones like he was looking for someone and his eyes connected with mine. His mouth didn't smile but his eyes did.

I couldn't help myself, I patted my hair. The motion of my hand made some of the others look over at me. One of them was Falcon's sister, Bernadette, Gentle Robin Wing, who was standing in front of Falcon so hadn't seen his eyes talking to mine. She didn't smile with her mouth or with her eyes so I thought a better name for her right then would be Fisher With A Sore Paw. She turned around to see who I had patted my hair for and grabbed hold of the arm of Sleeping Cougar and squashed her breast into it before she looked up at his face to see that he wasn't looking at me, but over into the forest. He had seen Paul Le Putois—or a part of Paul Le Putois—changing trees. I was so used to seeing Paul Le Putois's leggings in the most unusual places that I never paid attention anymore. Robin didn't see this but when Cougar motioned to Falcon that he should look into the trees, that something of interest, or perhaps concern, was going on there, Robin felt this movement and reacted. She also saw Falcon turning his head away from where I was. Then she looked at me quickly and I think she was in time to see the smile come out of my eyes because she moved her head downward a little bit and made her eyes close in a silent greeting. I did the same thing but then raised my chin up high and turned my face away. I didn't care if she liked that or not and I ran off to change my clothing.

The dress I wanted to wear would not fit around my hips anymore so my mother gave me one of hers which flowed around me like rapids around a rock. The beading and quillwork on it was beautiful. If I was going to be having a malie'wuti ceremony, a wedding, I would have to make my own dress for it and this meant I would have to put away my attitude and ask my mother how to do that kind of beading. I already knew how to do that kind of quillwork—we all did because of Young Rabbit Woman's mother. I didn't learn from her mother directly because she walked into the ocean three years before my mother had me, but I was grateful to her just the same.

In all the excitement of having visitors—and especially having Falcon smile at me with his eyes—I didn't notice that both Claude and Feather had disappeared.

Fourteen

As everybody had expected, Falcon did the best of everyone in three races, even the three-legged race with Atu'tuej tied to his leg, the two of them sounding like a pair of laughing-gulls the whole way across the clearing. Falcon came second in the knife throw but he was pleased to lose to his friend, Sleeping Cougar, the one who had taught him how to throw in the first place.

The women played the Bowl Game and Feather's team won over the rest of us. Gi'gwesu did third best in Snowsnake, the game with the long, long ice trough that stretched from our village to Falcon's village for sending messages back and forth and along which the participants would throw a spear. Everyone was surprised that Gi'gwesu did so well, but he was always good at learning things that used the body. I was proud of him and tried to hug him when I said it but he pushed me away and ran off with his friends.

The way we ran games in our village was to start out with the men and the women and end with the little ones and then the old ones. Doing it this way would show the little ones how to do things and then the old ones would remind everybody how it should be done, even though it was done slower. The Lnu Saqamaw of the other village told our Lnu Saqamaw, right in front of everybody, that he thought this was a very good idea and he would talk to his people about doing it our way when the summer came and we were invited to the gathering in their village.

We had finished with the races and the knife throwing and bow games and because the sun would soon be going down, we were heading over to the clearing near The Bear's Behind where there would be the singing and dancing around the sacred fire. Claude came running up to us, all out of breath and with steam coming off his clothes, and yelling.

"The levee," he said. "I just checked the levee…" He leaned over with his hands on his knees to catch his breath. "That leak… That little leak at the bottom… Getting bigger…Getting bad…"

The Lnu Saqamaw put his hand on Claude's back and leaned down. "Water coming in fast?" he asked. "Pushing out clay?"

Claude could only turn his head and look up into the Lnu Saqamaw's face.

"Little stones, too?"

Claude nodded. "Just a few… but…" His breath was hard to get. "And the tide will be high tonight…"

The Lnu Saqamaw left his hand on Claude's back as he turned to us, "We must tend to this immediately." He spoke again to Claude. "Are you going to be all right?"

"Yes," said Claude. "Quel désastre. Mon Dieu."

The Lnu Saqamaw moved away starting to organize things.

A movement on the path Claude had arrived on caught my eye. I expected to see a corner of Paul Le Putois there, being nosy as usual, but it was the Father, staring at me from behind the wide old mossycup oak there. I couldn't help myself, I gasped and this made Claude stand up straight and look at me. I pulled the top of my parka into a knot at my chest and I think my mouth fell open because Claude turned around quickly to look where I was looking, to see what had frightened me.

When his face turned back to me I knew that he knew. His eyes went wide and then narrow. "Ah," was all he said.

We both turned again but I couldn't even see the bright purple stripes on the edges of the Father's black dress, he had been that fast at moving away.

"*Forced?*" Claude stepped toward me with his arms out to hold me but was stopping and then starting again like a grouse drumming slowly.

"Don't touch me." This I said more to calm him than for my sake. I could have used a hug right then, especially from Claude.

"He's the one then." Claude turned again to look through the trees and then too loudly he said. "Je vais le tuer, I will kill him. Je le jure. I swear I will kill him."

"Don't," I said, my voice in a loud whisper, trying to make him quiet down. "I asked for it."

"Nobody asks for *that*." Then he made his voice lower, too. "Quand? When did it happen?"

"It doesn't matter. What matters is I am with child and I don't want to be his wife. I can't be his wife, he's a Father."

Claude didn't exactly laugh but the sound coming out of him was close to that. *Ha!* "No. Tabernacle. You won't be his wife. You will be *my* wife. I will marry you."

What came out of *my* mouth then was a laugh, though. "You're crazier than Paul Le Putois and Young Rabbit Woman put together."

"I promise I won't touch you. We will go to Oositookun across the basin. I know the priest there. He will understand. We will be married—"

"No, no, no," I said. "I don't want to marry you. You are my friend. I want to marry Falcon."

"Hear me out." He leaned in closer to me to whisper now but I could see that it was too late: Sleeping Cougar had been standing there the whole time.

I wondered if Sleeping Cougar had heard Claude's threat to kill the Father. That was what I was mostly worried about. But because Sleeping Cougar's face now looked like he had just tasted something awful, I feared also that I would not be getting Falcon as a husband. Sleeping Cougar stepped away to follow some of the people who were leaving to help repair the levee. Among them were One-Eyed Joe and his mother, a friend of Claude named Mathieu, and Young Rabbit Woman who was talking with Falcon and laughing—something One-Eyed Joe didn't like very much by the look of it—and Paul Le Putois who was, of course, not exactly with the group but was moving along behind the trees.

"Falcon," Cougar called out just before he turned to sneer quickly at me again. "Wait. I have something important to tell you." And he ran up to the group and started talking right away and pointing back at me and Claude. It wasn't just Falcon who was turning his head to see where Cougar was pointing, some of the others turned, too.

"I won't touch you," Claude repeated. "After the baby comes, after I give it a name, we will get an annulment. We will no longer be married then. It will be as though it never happened. We will both be free to marry another. If there is no consummation, there is no marriage."

"I know that but the widow of Martin Dugas—your betrothed—won't believe it. She will kill me. Apalqaqamej is right. I have to be careful around you. Especially now. With the rumors."

"Chipmunk is stupid. Don't believe anything she says."

"She is not stupid at all. She is actually very smart. She has no control of herself, that's all. What comes into her head comes out of her mouth. Don't be mean."

"You listen too much to gossip from the old women, as well. You believe everything they say. So does Chipmunk. I am not betrothed to Marguer—" He smiled at me and his eyes went to the side. "… to the widow of Martin Dugas. And she is not betrothed to me—"

"But you two—"

"Don't interrupt!"

"But—"

"She is no more betrothed to me than she is to anyone else. At least not right now. Do you not understand the difference between love and... Hé bien! Between love and just helping someone? Hé bien! How do I explain? She's a friend. That's what she is. A friend. I protect her."

"As if she needs protection," I said, pretty much to myself. "She's a strong woman. Forceful. No man who has a brain at all would be anything but afraid to do something to her. And she's almost as tall as I am."

"I protect her reputation."

I laughed at this but not because I was happy about any of it. "Her reputation doesn't need protecting either. She's the daughter of Catherine Bugaret!"

"That's why she needs protection," Claude said. "She's a lady."

I didn't understand this it all and my frown made Claude frown, too.

"She'll understand when I explain it to her. Just wait and—"

"I don't want his baby." I could feel my throat tightening up like it was doing a lot of lately. "Every time I look at it, I'll remember."

"We will solve that problem when the time comes. D'accord?" He patted my shoulder with the tips of his fingers and his arm stretched out as far as it would go and this made me laugh.

"I do love you," he said. "But not the same way I... Not the same way I love... Yes. I love her. You're right. I love Marguerite Petitpas, the widow of Martin Dugas. God knows I love her. And her children, too. Everybody else knows but her so I think she will soon have eyes for someone else. A friend of her father has a son who has been waiting to call on her when the time is right."

"And you are willing to take that chance for me? To sacrifice for *me*?" I found it both wonderful and hard to believe at the same time.

"For you. And for your baby. I must. You're my friend. I think of you as… as a little sister. You need protection, too. Marguerite is a grown woman. Like you said, she's strong. And not just physically. But if she rejects me—which may very well happen as her father's friend is influential both here and in Grand-Pré—I'll find someone else to be my wife…"

That won't be difficult, I thought, but of course I would never tell him *that.* It was hard enough to just think it. I couldn't imagine what it would be like if we couldn't be friends anymore, if he chose a woman who lived far away and had to be with her all the time.

"… if it comes to that. But it won't be you! Pas vraiment, not for real, at least. Mon Dieu, you're just a kid." He tried to say this last bit without laughing but the corner of his mouth twitched so I knew all was well between us once again.

"I don't blame the widow of Martin Dugas. I don't know anyone who would want to marry you and that makes me feel sorry for you, so I will marry you," I said to him, my smile wide. "But only until the baby gets here. Come on, let's go." I slipped my arm around his and pulled myself close to him. "They will need the help of everyone at the levee. Come on."

Claude patted my arm with his other hand and together we walked toward the path that led to the sea and the leaking levee. "We will go together arm in arm," he said. "That way, the announcement of our marriage won't be as much of a shock. I'll explain things to Marguerite. Maybe that will make me more desirable to her, eh bien? A gallant action is a trick that sometimes works on the heart of a reluctant woman."

"Eh bien," I replied, knowing that these gallant actions of his were certainly working on *my* heart.

As it turned out, we didn't go to Oositookun to get married. A priest came to us. Remember I told you our people have different meanings for the word disappeared? That it can mean it was on purpose or it was magic? We didn't know right away, of course, but later on we all found out that the disappearance of the Father wasn't anything to do with magic. Not at all. Yes. The Father disappeared. He didn't even get to help us with the levee but we were so busy nobody noticed who was missing and who wasn't.

☽ ○ ☾

With everybody helping, even the little ones, we got the levee fixed but it was dangerous doing it because some of us had to get wet. It was only a trickle of water slipping through from the basin, but if we left it until spring, it would have been what Claude said: un désastre. It would have gotten wider and wider and would have washed away a whole section of stones and sand and clay to flood the area with tide water every night while we slept. It was better we did it now even if it was wintertime. We all tried not to get wet but some of us did and the ground where we had to dig to get more clay and small stones from was frozen so we had to start a wide fire over it. Not an easy thing to do but that's how the little ones helped: they collected wood and twigs from under the snow and snapped them off trees if they were dry enough to almost fall off anyway and spread them around. Atu'tuej even offered the tamarack cones he had collected earlier for the children's tossing game but one of the older men told him to keep them, that they would only snap and make sparks. By sunset, everything was repaired but this left us no time for the dancing and singing so we all just went home to sleep, tired and dirty and cold. We would hold the rest of the ceremonies after Mass the next morning.

And Claude would speak to Marguerite Petitpas, the widow of Martin Dugas, the next morning, too, so he said, but I had my suspicions he would be telling her tonight when he was in her bed.

But the next morning, the people who always went to Mass came back to the village almost right away saying that the Father was gone.

"Gone?" said One-Eyed Joe. "Gone where?"

Nobody seemed to know but one of the men said he would go to the fort to tell them we probably needed a new priest. He'd heard that priests disappeared all the time. "Maybe they have a spare one at the settlement in Québec."

Claude's friend Mathieu was one of the coureurs de bois who had been helping us mend the levee and he had stayed overnight in the visitors' big wikuom. "They have enough of those bâtards there to fill both the hold and the deck of a cargo ship." He spat on the ground. "And it would be a crowded one. They have plenty of spares." I was surprised that he hated the priests so much but still went to Mass all the time. A lot of the coureurs de bois, even though many of them were always killing each other and stealing and drinking and fighting and taking our women, went to Mass when they could. I guess they were afraid of their god for different reasons than I could think of. Far as I could tell, though, Mathieu was a good man like Claude was. But like I said before, Claude didn't go to Mass very often.

Dancing Raven, one of the first of our men to help the Father with building his church, went to Mass all the time. He told us he got a bad feeling when he went to Mass that morning and the candles weren't lit so he and Mathieu went to check the Father's house.

Charles, a big coureur de bois, wide and fat and older than Claude by several years, was one of the men who had gone into the house with them. I didn't know him but it seemed that a few of the others did yet nobody wanted to talk to him. He poked Mathieu on the shoulder with his elbow. "Tell them."

I saw that Mathieu jerked away as if he didn't want to be touched by him but I couldn't tell if it was from fear or hate. Maybe both.

"What do you know that I don't know?" the Lnu Saqamaw asked the men and One-Eyed Joe grunted a question, too. But the question One-Eyed Joe grunted was to Mathieu, he made no eye contact with Charles.

They know each other from before somewhere. This started me thinking but I got distracted by what Mathieu said next.

"There was a pot of stew at the Father's fireplace and the fireplace was cold," Mathieu said. "And the stew already had a crust of ice starting on it." He put his head down.

Dancing Raven said, "The Frenchman killed him. Sleeping Cougar told us."

"Which Frenchman?" asked the Lnu Saqamaw.

"Claude Guidry, of course. The Woodsman. Sleeping Cougar heard him. 'I'm going to kill him,' he said. 'I swear,' he said." Dancing Raven, his face worried and serious, looked around at everybody. "He said it to her." And he pointed.

Everyone went really quiet then. Especially me.

Fifteen

We got our new Father in less than a moon and it seemed that spring soon followed him. He didn't come from the settlement at Québec but from near Mirligueche. His hair was gray which meant he was maybe forty or fifty summers old, but he was strong and lean—not like the other Fathers with their dresses tight over their bellies because of the food they ate—so he was able to help us with almost everything. He wanted us all to call him Père Gaëtan, even the little ones, and he was always smiling and very friendly with everyone. He was a good hunter, could gut a fish as fast and as clean as any of our men could and he ate the way we did. We all liked him, even me, but I was very surprised to learn that he knew Claude, too, from Saint-Malo. How was it that all the Fathers from the land of the King knew Claude Guidry? Claude had told me there were enough people in the land of the King to fill Isle de Chèvre at low tide, that nobody would be able to sit down and people would be falling off the edge of it, so how could Père Gaëtan know him so well?

I asked Père Gaëtan one day when I was visiting him at the house beside the church, the Father's old house, if he had known the Father, too. "He was also from Saint-Malo," I said. "That's what he told me once."

"Guillaume Soucy?" Père Gaëtan's laugh came out of his nose. "Guy was no priest!"

This was an even bigger surprise to me. Not so much that Père Gaëtan knew the Father on top of knowing Claude Guidry but that the Father had not been a Father.

"Close your mouth, Keskoua. You look like a baby robin about to fall out of its nest from reaching for the worm of gossip."

"The Father wasn't a Father? You mean he fooled us? Oh. Poor Feather. No wonder…"

Père Gaëtan leaned forward and whispered. "He followed Claude Guidry here." He leaned back, chin out. When he did this, he reminded me of some of the women Claude was always telling me not to listen to because whatever went into their ears came out of their mouths bigger, so I didn't really believe him.

"Why would he do that?"

"It's a very long story, Keskoua. Some of which I heard in the confessional so I will have to sort out what I heard inside the box from what I heard outside the box before I start tell—"

"Wait," I said. "You said Guy. Did you call him Guy?"

"I did."

"Did he know Madame? The wife of Philibert de Villegaignon, Marquis de Savoie? Claude's Madame?"

"Ah. So you do know the story." He seemed pleased—perhaps because I had saved him a lot of work thinking about what he had heard in the confessional and heard from outside it.

"Did he go to the banquets at the estate of Madame and the Marquis?"

Père Gaëtan smiled and nodded.

"And most important, did Guy love a young girl named Véronique? The niece of the Marquis?"

"One and the same," said Père Gaëtan. "One and the same. He was always a bit odd, you know. Most likely from losing his father and having an adulterous mother. The acorn does not fall far from the tree, you see." Père Gaëtan tapped the side of his head with his pointing finger.

I believed Père Gaëtan now. "I have to go." And I ran as fast as my baby-belly would allow me. I ran straight toward the house of Claude Guidry but on my way, I almost ran into Falcon coming around a corner in the trail.

"Keskoua," he said with no smile on his lips or in his eyes either and with Sleeping Cougar close behind him, staring at me, too. "The very woman I am looking for."

I think I screamed.

☽ ○ ☾

The next thing I knew, I was squinting up into the sky and Falcon and Sleeping Cougar were leaning over me like trees heavy with wet late-winter snow, frowns on their faces and whispering to each other.

"Do they do that when they're not going to have babies, too?" Sleeping Cougar was asking Falcon.

"I don't think so."

I opened my eyes wider and looked around, surprised to find myself lying on my back on a corner of the trail leading to Claude's house. "What?" I said, then I remembered why I had been rushing to see Claude—it was about what Père Gaëtan had told me about Guy and Claude—and that I had almost bumped into Falcon on the way.

"Oh, hey. Look," said Sleeping Cougar.

"Oh, good. Her eyes are open."

"Can she see us?"

"I think so," said Falcon. "She doesn't look… very happy. Does she?"

"I think you scared her."

"You think that's what happened?"

"Maybe, eh?"

"Stop talking about me like I was dead," I said. "Help me up." I lifted my arms up toward them and they each took an arm and lifted me to my feet like I was a piece of birch bark, they were that strong. I brushed off my arms and Falcon started to brush off my back but I stopped him when he got to my behind. "I'll do that myself." And I did.

"Sorry," they both said in unison and took two steps back each.

"Are you all right?" asked Cougar. "Like… You fell down, eh?"

"Yeah, as if you care." And I tried to give him the same look he had given me the day he had been listening to Claude and me talking about what the Father had done to me, that look that he had just bitten into something bad and rotten.

I guess I didn't do a very good job of it because Falcon stepped forward again and reached out to hold my elbow, a look of deepest concern on his face. "What's wrong? Are you in pain?"

"She's in pain!"

"What? No. Don't touch me." I wriggled away from Falcon's concerned grasp. "Go away. What do you want anyway?"

"I want to talk to you," said Falcon. "It's something important."

I crossed my arms. "I have nothing to say to you. And not you, either, Cougar. Go away. Both of you. I have things to do. I have something important to talk to somebody about. You aren't the only ones with important things to talk to people about, you know."

"We already talked to him," said Cougar. "The Frenchman, I mean."

"Yes, Claude Guidry," added Falcon. "The Frenchman. Your Frenchman. The Woodsman. La Verdure. We just talked to him. We're just coming from there now. We came looking for you."

"And there you were," said Cougar.

"Just like that."

"It's really important."

I held my chin up as far as I could and turned my face away from them.

"It's about the baby," said Cougar. "For one thing."

"It's about getting married to Claude," said Falcon. "For another thing. And for anoth—"

"You too?" I snapped at them. "I thought it was just the old women went around telling stories. I can't believe it."

"Don't forget I heard you two talking," said Cougar, his voice quiet and his eyes looking for something on the path.

"And of course you had to go and tell everybody what you heard!" I was angry and I wasn't going to keep it inside. "You made everybody think Claude did something bad to the Father, but he—"

"That's one of the things we went to talk to him about," said Falcon. "We found the Father."

"We were following a deer we got and it went out that way," said Cougar. "The deer led us to him."

"I missed the heart," Falcon said, his voice quiet now, too. "First time I missed the heart since I was a small boy."

"You found the Father. That's wonderful," I said, not caring a twig about the Father, only about the trouble Claude could get into if the Father was hurt or something worse. "Isn't it?

They didn't answer me and now Falcon was looking for something on the ground.

"What? Is he hurt?"

"He's at the bottom of The Bear," said Falcon.

"The Bear?"

"He maybe fell off it."

"Or he maybe jumped," said Cougar.

"Ridiculous," I said. "He's a Father. He would go to Hell if he jumped.

He wouldn't jump." But then I remembered what Père Gaëtan had told me, that the Father wasn't a Father after all. "Oh… Well…" I shrugged.

"Yes, yes, you're right," said Cougar, "So we think—"

"—we think he was pushed off the top," finished Falcon. "That's what we went to see Claude about. If he could come with us. He has good tools for climbing. We need to… You know… We can— Maybe he can—"

"The top of The Bear? Nobody goes up there." I was frightened now. For all of us. For the whole community. "Do you think Claude will go up there?"

"He can check for tracks. See if he can find out what happened."

"So…?" I was afraid to ask. "The Father is…?"

"He's a big mess," said Cougar. "Wolves got him before we found him. Tracks all over. It was a big pack and it looks like there were seven pups! A very large litter. It will be a good Rabbit Year. They kept coming back so tracks on tracks."

"How do you know he fell off The Bear then? If… You know… If there's not much left."

"Head smashed open on the rocks," said Falcon. "The wolves didn't do that. Even a little kid could see what happened even with the big melt the other day."

"Like a melon," added Cougar.

"All the way down. You can see…"

"Brains here on a rock, brains there on a rock and— Oh, sorry, Keskoua. I forgot you were… your condition."

This was one of the times I was not happy about having a good imagination and I don't think the baby liked hearing about its father this way because I felt it jump inside me and this time it made my stomach feel too full or something and that made a funny taste come into my mouth. "I'm coming with you," was all I said and I must have said it in a strong way because Falcon and Cougar didn't say no.

I started back the way I had come and they followed me. I didn't need to look back to know that Claude had joined us.

Along the way to The Bear, we decided we would all climb up its leg together.

☽ ○ ☾

Falcon, a rope in circles over one shoulder, led the way up The Bear's sticking-out back leg and Claude and Cougar followed close behind me and for that I was very glad when I reached the spot where the finger and foot holes ended, the ones that had been chipped into the rock by that unknown somebody many winters ago. While I was searching for a crevice to grab onto, something made my eyes turn toward the front of The Bear and that's when I saw its head and face looking back for the first time. And now I know why the unknown somebody stopped chipping holes up The Bear's back leg.

The look of such sorrow on the face of The Bear made me ashamed that I had been kicking my feet into the holes in its leg and digging my hands into it. It was like The Bear could see into the future and it was crying because of what it saw.

"Mesgei'," I said. "Mesgei', I'm sorry." And I started to cry so hard I slipped and nearly fell off the leg of The Bear. It made me wonder if that was what had happened to the Father, that he had looked into the face of The Bear and saw his future and fell off crying.

Claude caught my foot and held me up with it until I grabbed onto a stunted kaksk'us tree and was able to steady myself again.

The face was right there and had always been but I had never been able to see it, flat and round like the top of a stump and with its muzzle sticking out and its small dark round eyes on either side of that. The dark eyes were holes where water dripped through down the cheeks of The Bear.

Claude called up from below me. "Are you all right?"

This made Falcon turn around to look at me and I told him to keep going. "Don't look down or anything. Or sideways either. Keep going."

After Falcon got to the top, he went to a tree there and tied the finish-line rope that Feather and Atu'tuej and I had braided from the inner bark of a tall kaksk'us tree a moon ago. It felt like a life ago not a moon ago now. He threw the other end of the rope down and Claude tied it around my waist so Falcon could help pull me up with it. When I got up there beside him I went to the tree where the rope was tied and sat down behind it. The tears came so hard and from so far deep inside me and from so far ahead in my life that they made my whole body shake. I wondered if the baby inside me would be sad too and was crying in there.

Using the kaksk'us bark rope, Claude and Cougar got up onto The Bear's back with Falcon and me and they were talking and looking around and brushing dust and melting snow and things off their clothes so I knew they hadn't seen the face. Or if they had, they hadn't seen it crying. Staring at the ground, the men spread out and moved toward the middle of The Bear's back but I stayed where I was.

Spring was on its way so a lot of the snow up here had melted but you could still see that there had been tracks. Branches of pine and kaksk'us had been snapped or torn off by somebody and used to sweep the snow around so not even Falcon, Cougar and Claude all together could tell what had happened.

"Ça alors! Maudit. This proves it. Somebody pushed him off."

"E'e," Falcon agreed. "Yes. Why would somebody clean off their tracks before they jumped. Not up here. Nobody comes here."

Claude and Cougar grunted.

"No. Somebody did this to him."

Hand against a tree, Claude leaned over the side of The Bear to look down. "I see something." He leaned over even farther and I felt the baby jump so I stood up and joined the men at the edge of The Bear's back.

"What do you see?"

"I'm not sure," he said. "Get back, Keskoua. It's very steep. It's solid, but steep."

I looked around some more and could see that many of the trees had been here for a long time so they were starting to crack the rock with their thirsty and hungry roots. The rock was mostly smooth and roundish, like the wind had been blowing on it forever, but there were lines in it where dust and bits of plants and things camped and this is what the trees had decided to stand in.

"It looks like a bit of cloth. Or material of some kind," said Claude. "Take a look."

This he said to Falcon and Cougar as he stepped back and when he did, he took me by my shoulders and made me walk away several paces. "Not you."

"But I want to see."

"You're right," said Cougar. "It shines a little bit when the sun hits it. It could be a decoration from a woman's dress. What do you think, Keskoua? Do you recognize it?"

I pulled away from Claude so I could go see but he grabbed my arm to stop me. "You are not going near that edge."

"I climbed up here without any… Well, without much trouble." And I went to stand behind Falcon.

Behind me, Claude made a sound like his new breeding pig made whenever he put food out for her. I called this pig Gesm'pisit, which means strange clothes, because she had spots like her father but still had prickly hairs like her mother, Orignal-Sale, who was too old to have babies anymore. It was easier for me to get Gesm'pisit to do things than it was to get her mother to do them so I liked her a lot better than her mother, but I would still be very angry if Claude let Orignal-Sale get cut up for sausage.

When I told him not to do it, he crossed his arms and made his lips disappear inside his mouth but promised anyway to let her stay around. Then that annoying finger of his came out and shook at me when he said she would be the last one and that I had better understand that right now.

I was remembering this when I told him "You sound like Gesm'pisit when you do that snorting sound so stop it. I can hold onto the tree just as well as you can. If you're that sure I am too weak to stand here, then tie that rope around me."

Falcon went to get the end of the rope to tie it around me again and I was able to lean over to see what they were talking about. It was a piece of decoration, yes. But it was too far away to be able to see the details on it. "I can't tell from here," I said. "How can we get it?"

"How about a fishing hook?" said Falcon. "That would work. We could lower the rope down and see if we can grab it."

"I don't have a hook with me today," said Cougar.

Claude dug around in the pockets of his pants and shirt. "Me neither. Do you have anything that might work, Keskoua?"

I didn't.

"We have to come back then," said Falcon. "We'll get more rope and more tools. We'll get that thing. Somehow."

"I'll wait here," I said.

All three men said at the same time: "No you won't."

On the way back to Claude's house where he said he had plenty of fishing line and hooks, I told him I wanted to talk to him and I wanted to talk to him soon. My voice must have sounded angry because he stopped walking right there and Falcon almost bumped into him. Cougar bumped into Falcon.

"Quoi? What?"

"I said, I want to talk to you."

His hands went out like the Father's used to when he was praying out loud during the Mass. "Talk? About what? We have a serious matter to deal with here. What could be more important?"

"En privé, privately," I said, proud of the new expression I had learned from Geneviève, the mother of Paul Le Putois. She was teaching me French lately—and some of the other people, too. And how to read. She had "acquired"—another new word for me—several books from the fort and was teaching us how to read from them. I didn't much like the stories because nobody got what they wanted and all the women in the stories had to go away to convents all the time instead of getting married to somebody they loved. But learning to read and learning more and more new words was going to help me be a storyteller in more than my own language, so I was very happy to learn everything I could from Geneviève.

"Can't it wait?" Claude asked.

"Not really but I suppose I don't have a choice, do I?"

"Is she always this domineering?" asked Cougar.

Claude made a sound like Gesm'pisit and started walking again.

Later that day, we had our talk but not until after he explained what happened when they were climbing up The Bear again to get the piece of decoration.

Sixteen

On the way up The Bear's leg, Cougar, who was leading this time, looked over and saw the face of The Bear and slipped.

I don't know what went through his head because he wouldn't talk about it, at least nobody told me he did. I think if I had been Cougar, I would have talked about it all the time. The mother of One-Eyed Joe told us that talking about things that had frightened us helped keep them out of our dreams.

When Cougar slipped, there was nobody there to catch him like Claude had caught me so he slid down The Bear's leg right into Falcon. Falcon was not expecting this as he was right in the middle of reaching for his next handhold, so when Cougar slid into him, they both went to the bottom with Cougar on top. Claude was off to the side and even though he tried to grab them on the way by, he couldn't do it. He told me later that his first instinct was to catch them but that would not have been good because all three of them would have been injured and nobody would have been able to go for help. The clearing at The Bear was often used for special ceremonies and feasts but nobody much went around behind The Bear but Paul Le Putois. And he didn't do it every day.

As it turned out, Cougar got his face banged up pretty good and Falcon got one of the bones in the lower part of his leg broken. Claude said that my choice for a husband was a good one because even though the bone was sticking out, Falcon stayed calm and quiet and the only way you could tell that he was in pain was the wetness on his forehead.

Because he got his face banged up, Cougar was too dizzy to go to the fort for help so Claude told him what to do until he got back.

☽ ○ ☾

Falcon was lucky there was a fort nearby because at forts there was always somebody who knew how to look after injured soldiers so the médecin there would look after other people, too. If they asked him. When Claude came back to The Bear, he had four soldiers with him and half the village, including me. The soldiers lifted Falcon onto a special travois and started to go back to the fort. I wanted to come but Claude said I must not. Gi'gwesu and Atu'tuej said they would run to Falcon's village to let them know Falcon was hurt and Claude and Cougar, who was holding my shawl against his cheek, went with the soldiers and three of our men and Claude. They told everybody else to go back to the village and stay there, except for the mother of One-Eyed Joe.

By the time Falcon's parents got there, the mother of One-Eyed Joe had fixed up the big long cut on Cougar's face and the men were getting ready to fix Falcon's leg. They put the special travois on top of a strong table. I asked Claude to describe the surgical instruments he said were lying around all over the place but he wouldn't do it, just said he was happy to see the fort was so well-equipped to help people but even happier that he wasn't the one who needed the help. That was enough for me to stop asking him about them.

I was interested to hear about the rows and rows of brandy and wine and other bottles of drink and wondered how they could keep them safe from the coureurs de bois who sometimes ran out of money at the inn and started fights with the proprietor and stole bottles of liquor from there after the proprietor went to sleep. When somebody poured one bottle of it over Falcon's leg, it was all he could do, Claude said, not to cry out with the sting of it. Over on another table they were soaking strips of cloth in a basin of something Claude called "plaster." They would wrap Falcon's leg in these cloths to make a "cast" that would be as hard as a tree limb and would protect Falcon's leg while it healed. But first they had to hold him down, pull on his foot and fit the sharp bones back into the right places. One more soldier joined the group to make eight plus Claude and Cougar.

Two of the soldiers were trying to make Falcon drink what Claude said was "whiskey" right out of a bottle but Falcon was shaking his head and keeping his lips shut.

"If you don't want it, I'll drink it," said the stockier of the two soldiers. "Il est un bon Scotch whiskey de l'armoire du capitaine. Not like that merde they poured on your leg. This is good. Try it."

"He said no," came a voice from behind them. It was the father of Falcon. "He's a man. He can take a little bit of pain. Leave him be."

"I don't care how much of a man he is, no one can take the kind of pain he will be facing. And I don't think Hermel will agree to setting his leg without it."

"Who is Hermel?" The mother of Falcon stepped forward now. "And what is this Hermel going to do to my son?"

"Monsieur Hermel St-Amand—le médecin—is not going to do anything until that young man is unconscious. You are his mother. Tell him to drink the whiskey."

"He is a strong boy, my son. I am the one who is not strong enough to watch him in such pain." She turned to Falcon's father. "Tell him to drink it. Better drunk than dead and breaking my heart that way."

"Pain does not kill a man," said the father of Falcon. "You treat him like he's still on your teat, mother."

"I can do it, Father. You will be proud of me. I know you will." But as he said this, Falcon turned toward his father and this caused his leg to move. Claude could hear the bones grind together and almost cried out at the same time Falcon did.

Falcon's cry made his mother fall against the mother of One-Eyed Joe who almost fell, too, as she was quite old by now, but Claude was there to steady them both.

"Take what they are offering you," said Claude. "Don't drink it too fast or it will come right back up and you'll have to start over with the cheap stuff. It looks like it's the only good bottle they have so keep it down."

The father of Falcon snorted and left the room just as Monsieur St-Amand entered.

Monsieur St-Amand was from the land of Claude's King and because the mother of One-Eyed Joe trusted him and they often worked together, the mother of Falcon said he could go ahead and do what he needed to do. She wanted to stay to make sure everything went right but Monsieur St-Amand made her leave then turned to the mother of One-Eyed Joe. "We've done this together before."

The mother of One-Eyed Joe nodded and stepped in.

Falcon by now was starting to groan and the perspiration was running off him like he was a set of rapids. The stocky soldier put the bottle to Falcon's mouth again but Falcon pushed it away once more. The mother of One-Eyed Joe bent down close to him and whispered something in his ear and Falcon relaxed then, and began to drink. Because he was lying down, the first mouthful made him cough, said Claude, and he made an awful face and tried to get up on one of his elbows but this made him cry out so he lay back and turned his head to the side and drank from the bottle like a little baby at his mother's breast. After a short while, he started to talk about the deer whose heart he had missed with his arrow and then mumbled something like "She's a pain in the arse just like her name says but I love her anyway." And then he stopped talking and went into a special sleep.

Claude told me he didn't really want to tell me what Falcon had said about me, that it would be "plus romantique," more romantic, if Falcon told me himself, but Claude wanted me to feel better and not be so nervous about everything.

By this time, the men had gathered around Falcon so Monsieur St-Amand gave a signal and two soldiers and two of our men held Falcon's arms.

Four other men helped Monsieur St-Amand pull Falcon's leg way out to put the bone back inside the skin and then Monsieur St-Amand poured half a bottle of whiskey onto the leg.

"Waste of good whiskey if you ask me," said the stocky soldier. "Somebody already washed it out."

"They have discovered tiny creatures that hide inside wounds," said Monsieur St-Amand as he began to sew up Falcon's leg with special thread from the land of Claude's King. "My cousin, who has a great interest in science, has sent me what they call a 'microscope' and you can see these creatures when you look through it."

"Don't you mean a telescope?" said one of the other men. "What they use on ships and at forts, like ours here, to see into the distance?"

"Very much like a telescope, oui. But these instruments are used to see into another distance. The distance into small things." He had finished his sewing. "I will monitor the creatures that grow from his wound and the mother of One-Eyed Joe will take steps to eliminate them. Everything will turn out fine for young Falcon."

I wish I could tell you everything did turn out fine but it didn't.

Seventeen

One of the things that did turn out fine was that Claude talked to Marguerite Petitpas about me and she was very nice about the idea of us getting married for the sake of the baby. She even stood as witness for us at the marriage ceremony along with Claude's friend, Mathieu, and she let me borrow one of her very pretty dresses that she had worn when her own two babies were growing inside her. It was dark blue like a quiet pool of water in the moonlight and felt like the front leg of a lynx pelt when you rubbed your hand across it. After the ceremony, Claude, Mathieu and Père Gaëtan had all said it looked lovely on me and Claude told Marguerite that she looked lovely, too, and had winked at her.

I could hear the men toasting each other over by the gawatgw, the spruce tree, at the front of the church with wine that Père Gaëtan had provided as a wedding gift. We were standing under a big snawe'l, sugar tree, while Marguerite explained that the dress *she* was wearing was made from silk—she let me feel it (it was smooth and slippery and very shiny)—and was woven on a machine, un métier à tisser.

"Silk?"

"Well," she said. "You know what a spider's web is like and they make their threads inside their bodies and it comes out of their behinds."

I nodded. I had a feeling she wanted to keep me talking and away from Père Gaëtan in case I slipped up or something. Maybe she knew me better than I thought she did. Claude must have told her I had a habit of letting my thoughts spill out of my mouth like the tide leaving the basin. But she might have been trying to keep me away from Claude, too. After all, he and I had just gotten married to each other.

"… and a moth or a butterfly isn't a moth or a butterfly until they sleep in a *cocon*, a cocoon, made from inside their body, too?"

I nodded again. I knew all this of course but was wondering what else she could come up with to keep us talking until the men had finished drinking their wine.

"There's a moth that lives in a very faraway land called la Chine and when it's a worm and makes its cocoon, it is the softest, finest, shiniest thread you could ever imagine. There have been wars fought over this creature's silky threads."

This I didn't know.

"They can make many things from silk. See this scarf I am wearing?"

It was very pretty and matched her dress perfectly.

"That's one thing you can make from silk on a loom. Another is *velours*, velvet. The dress you are wearing is made out of velvet."

I felt my dress again. Soft. "Where can I get one of these métiers à tisser?" I asked her, all eager and thinking of the things I could make from one. I wondered if it would be easier than tanning a hide.

"I have a small one," she said. "I'll teach you how to use it. I also have a spinning wheel but to teach you how that works we nee—"

"You have a wagon wheel in your house that you spin sometimes?" This made me laugh to think of Marguerite walking up to it and spinning it for no reason. I had seen wheels on wagons at the fort and to me they were useless for anything other than moving something heavy from where the ships docked to the fort or back again. "Is yours some kind of toy?" I couldn't imagine having one in your wikuom or your house. For any reason.

Marguerite's smile was kind. "You're a very sweet girl. No wonder Claude loves you so much." She patted my cheek. "We need sheep for my wheel. I've been working on getting a ram and three or four ewes but—"

At my frown she explained that a ram was a male sheep and that females were called ewes. The offspring were called lambs and their meat was excellent. Meat from the older ones was also good but only if you cooked it right and used a lot of spices. The skins had many uses.

"Clothing, slippers, gloves…" she said, counting off on her fingers, then: "Feel my purse."

I did. It was almost as soft as her silk scarf.

"That's made out of sheepskin. Ha! They also use it to cover books, beds—Books and beds." She laughed. "Truths inside one and lies inside the other. Non? And we women never know which is which."

"I want to write books," I told her but she was off and talking and didn't seem to hear me.

"The ones not used for food are sheared each year for their wool and you spin that into threads that—"

She had my attention again. "Spin into threads?"

"Twist," she said and made her fingers rub together and moved them past her body to show me.

"On the spinning wheel we make the wool into fils de laine pour tricoter les vêtements, yarn to knit clothing. Their milk makes the most wonderful cheeses." She closed her eyes and turned her face up to the sky and clasped her hands for a moment as if she had stopped to pray. Then she looked at me with a sad face and waved her hands in the air. "We will have to wait a while before I can teach you how to spin wool and make things from it—and make cheese. I have asked at the fort to be informed the next time a shipment arrives. 'A shipment' they call it." She laughed then leaned in to whisper to me. "I understand there is a large and very secret economy flourishing in The Colonies regarding sheep and the products of sheep. But the way things are between New England and our people these days… I don't know." She waved her hands around again. "Men are always fighting with each other. And England is so controlling! Imagine. Not allowing your own people to knit! Not allowing them sheep in The Colonies! Being greedy over money is bad but fighting is worse. Wars are dreadful. Terrible things. But of course there are always exceptions. Right? War against les maudits anglaises est toujours acceptable. Always justified against the English. Oui?"

"Maybe Claude can get you some sheep. He—"

At the mention of his name, I saw Claude turn to look at us but with a flick of her hand, Marguerite dismissed him and turned me so my back was facing the men. "The English are so selfish. Even toward their own colonists. I wouldn't be surprised if they carry through their threat to separate. I—" She shook her head and asked quietly. "Claude? What was that you say about Claude?"

"Maybe he can get you some sheep. He knows people."

"Ha. You may be right. Perhaps I will ask him to look into the matter, but right now…" She tapped my baby belly with her finger. "His mind is occupied elsewhere. Come along now." She grabbed my arm to lead me away while Claude, Mathieu and Père Gaëtan continued to chat and sip on wine in the background. "Claude?"

Claude raised his glass to show it was almost empty and this meant he would be following us soon.

"You could ask some of the coureurs de bois to see what they can come up with next time they visit The Colonies. They bring back all kinds of things."

"They *steal* all kinds of things, ma chérie," she said, leading me along the path to her house. "If I can't get sheep through ah... legitimate means... only then will I ask the runners what they can do for me. D'accord?"

As we walked, we passed a field patchy with little white flowers. "The atuomgoming are starting to be ready," I said, my mouth filling with water thinking about crushing them and spreading them out in the sun to dry and their sweet-sour smell filling my nostrils and then my mouth. "Oh! I think I need to ask around the village if anybody has some dried atuomgoming from last season."

"That's... raspberries?"

"Strawberries."

"Of course. Atuomgoming." She rolled the word around her tongue. "Strawberries. Best cooked in pastry if you ask me. With lots of sugar. Wonderful, wonderful sugar."

I groaned in agreement. Another of the best things the Newcomers had brought with them was flour. Because of flour, making our lusgnign, our bannock, was a lot easier and they had showed us many other things to make with flour, like pastry—pies. Strawberry pie. Now I was even more certain that I wouldn't be able to wait until there were enough berries for pie so I tried to take my mind off my strong desire for atuomgoming until I could ask around for a piece of it dried. "Where are we going?"

"We can't expect a young woman who is close to delivering her baby to live in that shack Claude calls his home. And with its single bed. Nothing more than a bag of chicken feathers on the floor. Can we? You two will be moving in with me."

"Oh."

I was excited to know that I would be learning some interesting skills like spinning and knitting and making pies, but I was just as excited to know that I now had a new friend even though she liked to make people do what she wanted them to do. I didn't think she would have any trouble at all getting her sheep. What people had said about her was true then, and I felt a lot better about Claude wanting to be with Marguerite Petitpas now that I knew her better. She was a good woman. Thoughtful. With good morals and strength of character. She would be the best one for Claude. It seemed that he was a lot smarter about women than I had thought he was.

Claude told me it was usually two men who stood as witness to a marriage but that he had received special permission from Père Gaëtan to have Marguerite be the other witness. I somehow knew that was because Père Gaëtan didn't dare say no to Marguerite Petitpas. The more I got to know her, the more I realized that nobody wanted to say no to Marguerite Petitpas. Even though she was like that, she did it in such a kind way that most of the time you didn't even notice because she always had good ideas about how to make things work out for people—other people, not just herself—and they all ended up happy about it. For one thing, she made it look like it was all three of us, and not just her, who decided that it would be best if we didn't tell Père Gaëtan that we planned to get the marriage annulled as soon as the baby came.

"He wouldn't be able to perform the ceremony in all good conscience," she told me. "When you make the promise 'I will' at a marriage ceremony, you are supposed to mean it at the time or else it's a sin. A lie." She shook her finger at me. This made me wonder if Claude had learned this from her or if she had learned this finger-shaking habit from Claude. "Please promise me that you will never let anybody else know that you two told a falsehood to a priest in the house of God."

I promised even though everybody already knew anyway. Except Père Gaëtan, that is.

"God will understand," she said. "You are doing this for the future of the child. If there is one thing worse than a bastard in this world, it's a half-breed bastard." She patted my cheek again. "You are not as dark as some of your people so let's pray that the child turns out to be light skinned. You still want to give it away, n'est pas? I could never do that. What if you change your mind later? Start to miss it?"

"I won't miss it. I don't even want—"

"I know, I know, ma chérie. It will only serve to remind you of a terrible experience. Claude told me. And Geneviève told me, too. Heaven knows *that* poor woman knows what it's like to be forced to—"

"Geneviève? What does Geneviève know about anything?"

Marguerite tilted her head to look at me from under her eyebrows then raised one of them.

"E'e. Paul Le Putois," I said.

"What do you expect from him? He loves you, you silly goose. Didn't you know that? Geneviève told me he was completely distraught about what that beast did to you. You think *Claude* wanted to kill Guy Soucy? Ha! It was all Geneviève could do to stop her *son* from tearing him apart with his bare hands. 'You have enough killing on your soul,' she told him. 'Let somebody else do it this time.'"

"Really? She said that?"

By this time we had reached Marguerite Petitpas's house and I had to admit that she was right about having me and Claude move in with her. Her house had a shining floor made of wood and three separate sections with walls up to the ceiling and every section had a big soft bed with—yes, with what I knew had to be sheepskins covering each one—and chairs, and wooden boxes with "drawers" to keep things in. These boxes with drawers she called "bureaux." The beds looked warm and soft. I would sleep well here. With the baby getting bigger and bigger, I was finding the kaksk'us and skins on my side of my family's wikuom to be thinner and thinner no matter how high I piled them.

Nobody said anything when Claude and I started living in Marguerite's house. They all knew what was going on. Père Gaëtan kept trying to get me alone and I know it was to ask me what I was thinking of by getting married to the man who was the father of my baby and then moving in with his lover and her two children along with him, but wanting to give away my own baby. It was funny if you thought about it from Père Gaëtan's side of things—not knowing the truth, I mean—but not if you were Père Gaëtan. I kept telling him "Oh, I'm sorry but I'm busy right now," and "Oh, I have to go and do this or that," and "Oh, I just remembered I have to go and see somebody." For a while he believed me but then he finally gave up and stopped asking me altogether.

I think he was angry but I didn't really care because my main worry by now was for Falcon. This was one of the things that didn't turn out fine.

Falcon's leg was healing and this made it hurt more. Monsieur St-Amand explained that it was "knitting". This was not quite the same kind of knitting that Marguerite had told me about, but the word was a good one to mean doing either one of those things—and this could last for a whole moon, maybe less, maybe more. At first, Falcon was only drinking liquor when the pain got too bad for him but the closer it got to my wedding day with Claude, the more often Falcon was drinking and he even moved to our village because—he said it like it was a joke, the same kind of joke the coureurs de bois drinkers used—"It was closer to the inn at the fort. ha ha." My little brother, Gi'gwesu, told me that Falcon wanted to be closer to *me*, not the fort, but didn't know that and that's why he kept drinking more and more so he could stop himself from finding out and being extra sad. Gi'gwesu warned me that Falcon's drinking would get even worse after the wedding. Gi'gwesu had had a dream.

Gi'gwesu was right. Falcon would get drunk enough to go into that special sleep both in the mornings and in the afternoons now, but it seemed that it didn't work at night, though. He would be awake until the moon was as high as it could get, and be hollering and crying out loud and singing and—like I said, he couldn't dance because of the hard plaster on his leg but he would try anyway and often fall over laughing at his own stupidity. Our people never laughed at him and if somebody saw him like that they would try to help him get up on his feet again and try to get him to go to his wikuom to sleep, but the coureurs de bois and those of our men who got drunk, too, would laugh along with him. They were such drunks themselves that they thought he was doing it on purpose to amuse them like he used to do before his spirit got broken along with his leg. Sometimes they would be so selfish, they would just leave him lying beside the path and walk away to do what drunk people did. It was springtime now so not so cold for sleeping outside without covering your body or without shelter, but in the morning he would be sick from the liquor and sick from the bugs that had been biting him all night.

Falcon had no reason to worry about me and Claude because Claude was true to his word and never tried to get me to consummate the marriage—even though he never got the chance anyway, Marguerite was always around me whenever he was—but he did give me a kiss on the lips after Père Gaëtan said "I now pronounce you man and wife," but not right away.

As soon as Père Gaëtan pronounced us, I moved away toward where Marguerite had been standing, but she had already stepped in close to Claude where she whispered. "Try to make it look like you love each other. Don't you think?"

I heard her so I moved close to Claude again.

"Kiss her," Marguerite whispered.

"Quoi?" said Claude, stepping away from both of us. "In the church?"

"What better way to seal a contract?"

I was surprised to see that Père Gaëtan had a big happy smile on him when Claude leaned in with his lips sticking out like a moose reaching for a stem of swamp grass and he said, "She's not your sister, Claude Guédry!

She's your wife now. You can give her a good one." Then he laughed.

Claude and I pretended to laugh along with him. "It's all about respect. Isn't it Keskoua? I mean Marie-Thérèse." And he winked at me. "*Madame* Marie-Thérèse maintenant. Oui?"

Young Rabbit Woman, the mother of One-Eyed Joe, Geneviève and my mother had prepared a feast for after the marriage ceremony and the whole village and everybody from the village of Falcon and Cougar gathered in the clearing near The Bear and we all had a good time dancing. Even me, although I had to dance like a Grandmother, barely moving my feet, because of my baby-belly. Claude was watching me from one of the seats and laughing at this all the while with his arm across the shoulders of Marguerite who was leaning against him. Nobody seemed to notice or care about this, especially Falcon, who was almost falling over by this time with the drink. The only one who was frowning was Père Gaëtan who kept trying to ask people questions about what was going on with me and Claude and Marguerite but nobody would answer him, they would just try to hide their smile and would walk away laughing.

Falcon was the best dancer I had ever seen but of course he couldn't dance now. He was sitting over at the side with the little children and I could tell he was very unhappy about not being able to dance and about it not being our own wedding because he wasn't even moving his one free foot or his head, he was just there looking sad. Feather kept bringing him something to eat or drink and she would put her body in between him and me so we couldn't see each other. He would lean forward on his elbows sometimes or lean back pretending to stretch his good leg out but she would move, too. I knew she was giving him more liquor than food and that was not because she wanted him drunker (or maybe she did) but because she wanted to show him she would make a good wife by doing things she thought *he* wanted whether they were good for him or not. I thought this was really stupid because if you loved your man, you wanted the best for him so you might try to stop him from doing things that might end up killing him. Life was hard enough without doing dangerous things on purpose. I guess this is one of the things she learned from the Father and decided to hold onto: that God would only kill you when it was your time to go, and that the man was the head of the house and had to be obeyed no matter what. With our people, the woman had just as much say as a man did. Sometimes more if he wanted to get something from her that she didn't think was right to give. Over behind the trees I could see Paul Le Putois not exactly dancing but keeping time to the music and I thought this was strange. Not because Paul Le Putois was almost dancing but because he looked happy. I had never seen him looking happy and I don't think anybody else ever did either. It looked funny to see how his face wrinkled where it had never wrinkled before. The happy man was sad and the sad man was happy. Funny how things worked out sometimes.

I was surprised to learn that Cougar was such a good singer. He joined our men around one of the big drums and sang along with them for a long time and he even taught them two new songs that he learned when he was in Mirligueche in the summer.

Something else I noticed was the way Cougar kept trying not to look at The Bear. When he first sat down to drum, there was an empty spot that would put his back toward The Bear but he made our men move over so he would have The Bear, not in front of him—*No, no,* he said with his head, not that seat and not that one—but to the side so he could see anything coming from his eye's corner. When Paul Le Putois's shadow had first come out from behind The Bear, I saw that Cougar missed a drumbeat with his stick and his face lost its color, and his color didn't come back until they got almost finished with the next song. Would we ever learn where that piece of decoration hanging off the side of The Bear had come from? I didn't think it would be through Cougar we would get the answer.

I thought of going to Paul Le Putois to get him to climb up The Bear to get the piece of decoration. He was crazy enough to do it by himself and because he was not one of our people, he maybe wouldn't even notice The Bear's face and what it looked like and how it made you feel. But I also wondered: What if he was the one who killed the Father despite his mother's request not to? That would make four men dead by Paul Le Putois's hand if he did it, maybe more. I would have to find another way to get the piece of decoration.

Another thing that didn't turn out fine was when, a little more than a moon after the wedding, Gi'gwesu came running up to Marguerite's house to tell me that nobody could find Falcon. And that Paul Le Putois was nowhere to be seen either. And nobody could find Paul's mother to ask her.

. . . and had I seen Feather.

"Is she missing too?"

"No. Somebody at the fort wants to see her."

"Nothing new there," I said.

Gi'gwesu shrugged. "It's her soldier. He came back."

This is when it felt like somebody stabbed me in the back. My baby was coming. And my baby was coming early.

Eighteen

Having a baby didn't hurt as much as I had prepared myself for. A lot of the women had told me it would be the worst thing I ever went through and one of them said it would be enough to make me never want to lay with a man again. I didn't tell her that I already felt that way about laying with a man. Having the baby did hurt, I don't want to tell you it didn't, but it felt like a natural hurt, not when I cut myself or banged my knee on a stone or something.

The thing that hurt more than anything I could have imagined was when I looked at the baby's face (it was a girl) and even though her face was red and squeezed up like she was in the bright sunlight, I thought she was the most beautiful thing I'd ever seen. Her hair was black and stiff and straight and when her face opened up to look at me I could see that her eyes were big and blue. It wasn't easy for me to say "Take her away."

The mother of One-Eyed Joe was very good about it and she covered the baby with a deerskin blanket quickly and took her away to Second Son's woman because Apalqaqamej had enough milk for both her own baby and for this new one. My mother and Marguerite helped to wash me and they put me in a clean bed and brought me a special drink we all called gagîge'bûg water even though the word didn't come from our own language. It was something our women took after their babies were born.

When the mother of One-Eyed Joe came back she had a pouch full of dried sage for tea and she handed this to Marguerite but spoke to me. "This will dry up your milk when it comes in," she said. "Six times a day for as long as it takes. And something else…" She looked straight at me with very serious eyes and my mother and Marguerite stopped what they were doing and turned to look at me, too. "After maybe a few days, maybe a moon, maybe two moons, if you start to feel really sad or stop liking things, you need to come and talk to me or your mother—"

"Or me," said Marguerite. "I had it for a couple of days after my Abraham was born so I know what it feels like."

"Yes. Or Marguerite, too," said the mother of One-Eyed Joe, agreeing. "She will be a good one, too. You need to remember one important thing. It is normal for a woman to go through this after their baby is born so do not think it's because you gave your baby away."

Their faces were so serious that it scared me a little bit so instead of saying yes, I just nodded my head without a smile or anything.

"Don't forget," my mother said.

I shook my head to tell her I wouldn't forget.

"Don't forget," said the mother of One-Eyed Joe and Marguerite together.

I shook my head again.

The next day, Claude and Marguerite came into my room to say that the baby was doing well even though it had come early so was small, and this is when Claude told me that he and Marguerite were going to name the baby Jeanne Guédry dit La Verdure and that it would be baptized and that Jeanne de la Tour (that's where the name Jeanne came from, he told me) and Marguerite's father (called "Claude," too) would sponsor her and the baby would be coming to live with Claude and Marguerite and her two babies when it was weaned and that was that and they would not hear any argument from me.

"What's one more?" Claude said, smiling at Marguerite and referring to her two small children.

When I made the decision that I didn't want the baby because it would always remind me of what the Father had done to me to put the baby inside me, I wasn't thinking. I said I wanted to give it away but to where? It would have been to somebody in our village so I would have to always look at it anyway. I didn't think of this when I yelled at Claude and called him some bad names in my language.

He looked at Marguerite then. "You were right," he told her. Then he looked at me and said "I'll talk to you when you are feeling better, Keskoua." Then back to Marguerite again: "I have something to do. You explain it." And he left.

"Explain what?" I asked. I was very angry by now still thinking that somehow giving up my baby would mean she would be far away from me and this is what I had wanted but it was looking like that would not happen. I had not thought it through. I was usually really good at thinking things through but when you are with child your thinking sometimes doesn't work the same. I was angry with myself, not with anybody else, but sometimes my anger spilled out on anybody standing close to me. Just ask Gi'gwesu about that. I was always doing it to him. "Explain what?" I asked her again.

"What did you think, Keskoua? That we would take the baby out into the bush and leave it there for the spirits or whatever you people think comes to get them when you abandon your babies like that?"

I was so shocked that she would say such a thing as "you people" that my anger ran away from me and hid somewhere for a few moments. My mouth must have dropped open because she touched me under my chin and lifted it up. Water was getting ready to climb up into my eyes and I knew she couldn't miss seeing that because she was staring right into them.

"I'm sorry, Keskoua, but is that what you were thinking? You wanted us to let your baby die? Just throw it away into the bushes?"

I twisted my head away from her finger and her eyes. "Uh. No. I..."

"We couldn't do that. We're civilized people." She turned my face to hers again.

"What do you mean 'you people'? Our people don't throw babies away."

She let my face go and stepped back, crossing her arms. "Father Soucy once told me—"

"Father Soucy is a liar!" I screamed at her. "*Was* a liar," I corrected myself but this made me laugh and when I laughed my empty baby-belly began to jiggle and the more I tried to stop it by holding it with my hands, the more I laughed and the worse it jiggled. "Oh, stop." I yelled.

By this time, Marguerite was smiling—although she was trying hard not to—and Claude was suddenly standing at the doorway to the room with a scraper in one hand and a smooth wooden board in the other.

"Tabernacle. What's going on in here, hostie?"

Marguerite clucked her tongue. "Watch your language."

"Mon Dieu, I can hear you clear outside in the woodshed. Tabernacle. The noise. A-t-elle perdu la tête? Has she lost her mind?" This last to Marguerite. "Is this what happens to women when they give up their baby? Sacrément." Then to me, "Have you lost your mind?" But it seemed that my laughter had also affected Claude because the side of his mouth pulled up and soon he and Marguerite were laughing along with me.

When we calmed down, Claude waved the wooden board at me. "This is the last piece for the baby's bed. I will finish it today. Do you want to see it before I paint it?"

In one way I wanted to see it to make sure it would be a nice one for the baby but for the same reason, I did not want to see it. "Maybe another day." And I rolled over onto my side. "Let me sleep now."

And I slipped away into a very bad dream about me, Falcon, Cougar and Claude throwing the Father and his baby off the back of The Bear while Paul Le Putois stood at the bottom yelling up at us that he would catch the baby. I woke up before he caught her so didn't know if he did or not, and water was running off my body and out of my eyes and my breasts were pinching and hurting something terrible. I struggled out of bed to go to the fireplace in the room Marguerite called la cuisine, the kitchen, but when I got there I saw that the kettle was already steaming. What looked like porridge bubbled in a pot hanging on a hook in the fireplace.

"You were having un cauchemar, a nightmare. You were making an awful noise. Do you want to talk about it?" She looked at my face then at my chest. "Ah, your milk has come in. Does it hurt yet?" Then she had a cup in front of her and was spooning dried sage from the pouch that the mother of One-Eyed Joe and brought for me.

I looked down to see that the front of my gown was wet at my breasts. "Yes. It stings something awful." I put my hands on my breasts and I was surprised to feel that they were very hard and hot. "Will the tea help?"

"Sit."

Now Marguerite was telling me to sit. I still wasn't used to tables and chairs. For my whole life I sat cross-legged on kaksk'us boughs or on split logs sometimes. I pulled the chair back and it made a horrible scream on the floor. "Sorry." I wasn't sure if I said that to Marguerite or to the chair, but I went ahead and lowered my behind onto the seat but my knees ended up high, almost bumping the table.

"What's wrong with the table?" I asked. "And this chair?" I bent over to look underneath the chair and saw fresh marks on the bottom of the legs.

"The table was wobbly."

"Yes. I know," I said. "But…"

"So Claude tried to even it up by sawing a bit off its legs." She was trying not to laugh. "Then he had to saw them off again."

"This chair, too?"

"All of them. With the table so low, he…"

She couldn't finish so I did. "He shaved off the chairs too."

If I wasn't so tall, it might have been comfortable. I leaned forward to rest my arms on the table.

She poured hot water from the kettle into the cup but before she set it in front of me, she said "It is not considered polite to put one's elbows on the table."

"Oh." And I sat up straight and reached down to grab the chair, ready to shuffle it forward so I could pick up my cup of tea but the angle, with my knees way up now, made it difficult.

"Let me show you what they do at the aristocratic banquets of France," she said. "Claude showed me." She walked around behind me and grasped the back of my chair in both hands. "A gentleman helps a lady get closer to the table by standing behind her and moving the chair as she sits up off it a bit."

I put my legs out to the side and tilted myself up and forward then shuffled ahead like an old Grandmother dancing, while she pushed the chair along below me. The chair cried out once more. I was used to balancing the extra weight of the baby in front, so I put my hands out ready to catch the edge of the table if I lost my balance.

"Don't use the table for support, ma chérie. You need to learn how to do this gracefully."

"Gracefully?" I looked like a toad in mid jump. "How do you people do it with all those dresses on?" I asked, realizing at the same time as she did that I had said "you people." I started to laugh and this made me fall back onto the seat of the chair. It would have tipped over with my sudden weight on it if Marguerite had not been there to steady it. "I need more practice."

"You most certainly do. And did you hear yourself? You said 'you people.' You said 'you people.'" She managed to get this out from between laughs. "You need a lot more practice. We'll have Claude help you learn how. He is more experienced with getting ladies' arses into and out of chairs than I am."

And of course this set us off again.

Nineteen

One of the other men Feather got involved with right about the time of the dancing and singing ceremonies—and why she disappeared around the same time that Claude went to check the dikes that time, and why she didn't learn for such a long time that her soldier had returned for her—was the one they called Fou-Fou Fernand. Fernand was gentle with her at first, even though he was more attentive than she would have liked, but he had "fallen in love with her immediately" (so he said) and loved her so much that she would have to understand why he was jealous of the other men—"especially of Paul Le Putois" (this last, I found really hard to believe). Within a moon, he was screaming at her and threatening to cut her throat if she strayed more than a few trees away from him even to relieve herself. On the urgings of Paul Le Putois (maybe Fou-Fou Fernand had been right?), the other men "had a talk" with him and suggested he might find better furs up north. At least as far away as Hochelaga, hein? Maybe better would be as far away as Chaudière Falls, peut-être. Best might be as far away as that new maudit anglais fur-trading company everyone was talking about. They left the choice up to Fou Fou but insisted it be far away and that he should get there as fast as he could.

Fou-Fou Fernand came to Feather shortly after "the talk" with both eyes yellow and blackening and his nose off to the side, limping, and holding the side of his chest when he talked. "I have to leave. Pressing family business."

She could see that Paul Le Putois and two other runners were watching them from the trees and that Fou-Fou kept glancing over at them, scared half to death.

"He didn't even kiss me goodbye," she said. "He just shouldered his pack and walked away into the bush."

"It would have gotten worse over time."

"That's what Paul told me. Said his father was like that."

"He remembers?"

"People think Paul Le Putois is stupid."

I laughed and so did she.

She got very quiet and I knew she was then remembering André who had treated her so very well just before she had gotten mixed up with Fou-Fou. André had taught her things about the bush she hadn't even known herself. He had traveled with a great explorer, he called him, a man called Pierre-Esprit Radisson, so had seen many things and many people but André was old and slow by the time they met.

"I wish I had known he was dying…"

"There is nothing you could have changed."

Her head went down.

"Talking helps."

So she talked but it didn't help and I knew her mind was going even farther back—to François d'Orléans, her soldier. André had been the closest kind thing to her soldier but he had died and she was alone again. And now she had returned to the village.

It was time now for me to tell her that her soldier François had come back to settle in Acadia, had already built a house, and was looking for her.

After I told her that, she refused to come out of her wikuom for three whole days, not even to prepare food or relieve herself. She wouldn't even speak to me until I forced myself into her wikuom on the fourth morning.

"You have to stop this, Hélène," I told her, using her church name. "You will have to face François eventually so you might as well get it over with now."

"What have I done, Keskoua? What have I done?"

"You did nothing," I told her. "It was all done *to* you. Even what your soldier, François, did was done to you."

"How can he ever love me when he learns that I have been with others?"

I couldn't believe that the not-a-Father Father Soucy's influence was still stuck in her brain like a shelf fungus on a tree's trunk. "You have to get that nonsense out of your head. It was you he loved, right? Not your actions. You."

By this time, my brother Gi'gwesu and a couple of the other younger people had arrived at the door flap to Feather's wikuom and were handing food in. I took it and placed it on the kaksk'ug in front of her. She looked at it but didn't touch it. Another hand entered with a container of water. This she accepted and drank like she hadn't had any water in days. Which she hadn't.

She burped. "Do you think he still wants me?" she asked, reaching for the food the young ones had brought for her. "What is he going to do? Will he be like Fou-Fou and accuse me every day of infidelity just because I was not a virgin for him?"

"Fou-Fou was an idiot. And your soldier came back to you, didn't he? Fou-Fou didn't." At this I closed my eyes and thanked Kji Niskam. For both things.

She nodded, her eyes still puffy from days of crying but with a glint of hope in them now. "Do you think so?"

"I heard he took hunting lessons when he was in the land of Claude's King. So that means you and your children won't starve to death after all."

Her laugh was weak, but it was still a laugh. Maybe I would end up being a good Grandmother after all.

Twenty

Things settled down quickly at Marguerite's house and Père Gaëtan said he would be more than happy to arrange an annulment for us. He sent off a letter to the Bishop at the settlement of Quebec. "I know he will grant it for my sake but you have put me in an uncomfortable position. I should never have allowed the ceremony in the first place. I should have known better." He twitched his mouth at Claude. "At least with Madame Marguerite there at all times…" He twitched his mouth at Marguerite. "… we are assured that the marriage was not consummated. Oui?" He twitched his mouth at me. I just rolled my eyes.

I was still angry that Marguerite and Claude would be taking Jeanne into their house to live with them but my anger was not as strong as before, so when I told Claude I would be moving back to the village to be with my own people, I was as sad as he was.

"You might as well stay until the Baptism…" His face wasn't showing anything but I knew him well enough to know he meant it. "I'm going to miss you. You've been more like a daughter to me than ever by living under my roof." He hugged me. It was the first time we had ever been close physically like that and it felt good to be in his arms.

So that made two reasons I couldn't keep living with him and Marguerite. I think I loved him the way she did now and also, she was making plans for the baby's ceremony at the church and piling up decorations and baby clothes everywhere—even in my room—and having her sisters knit booties and bonnets and soakers. The air was full of baby, baby, baby and this made my heart full of no baby, no baby, no baby.

"No. I must leave."

And I did. I went back to my family's wikuom and changed all the kaksk'ug on my side and gave away all the reminders of Claude and the baby and smudged inside and outside the wikuom with sweetgrass and tobacco and smudged the wikuoms beside ours and was about to start smudging the wikuoms beside the ones beside ours when the mother of One-Eyed Joe came up to me and put her hand on my wrist to lower my smudge pot.

"Stop."

My eyes met hers and I threw my arms around her, dropping my smudge pot as I did so and I cried and cried and cried. My mother and Geneviève came up to us and put their arms around us. One of the young boys, it could have been Gi'gwesu but my eyes were so full of water and sadness I couldn't see who, took the smudge pot away and took care of the embers.

I was having that sadness they had told me about—and I was worried about Falcon, too—so the mother of One-Eyed Joe told me I had to do something to take my mind away somewhere else or the sadness would stay longer.

☽ ○ ☾

I decided I would do my best to learn who had killed the Father so talked Sleeping Cougar into going with me to The Bear to get the piece of decoration. I knew I would recognize where it came from as soon as I saw it. There were still a lot of people who didn't believe us about the cloth and thought we were trying to keep Claude from getting in trouble. Half the village thought it was Claude for sure who had killed him, the other half changed back and forth between Paul Le Putois and the Father himself. For me, I didn't want to think it was Paul Le Putois, but I couldn't help myself.

I don't know how we did it and Cougar doesn't know how we did it because I didn't want to go and neither did he—we were both terribly afraid—but Cougar and I decided we would go up onto the back of The Bear and solve the mystery once and for all.

We borrowed a rope—a very long one—from the fort and a few other things we might be needing and off we went without telling anybody where we were going. It was going to be difficult enough without having a lot of opinions following us around.

"If we get through this," Cougar said. "I will want to ask you something. Well... First I need to tell you something. I love Robin, the sister of Falcon, and with a little work on my part, I know I could persuade her to come live with me, but Falcon is my friend. He would want me to make sure you are safe and happy and well looked after."

I was too surprised to say anything and I think he appreciated this, taking my silence for consideration. Obviously he didn't know me very well.

"Besides, he has taken to the drink of the White man so he is lost. You don't want him, Keskoua. I will be good to you."

I didn't answer. I couldn't. I was here at The Bear trying to take my mind off Falcon and here was his best friend bringing Falcon to stand beside us.

"I'm sorry," he said. "I'm sorry. I... Forgive me."

"Of course. But only if you tell me what you saw before you fell off The Bear." I smiled at him so he would know I was teasing. But I was serious, too. I liked Cougar but not the same way I liked Falcon. And if something happened to Falcon that I couldn't be his woman, I couldn't go with Cougar. It would remind me of Falcon all the time. It seemed to me right then, that I was going to have to learn how not to be reminded of something all the time, but to instead just get over things and move ahead in my life. We have four hills to climb in our lives and it's not good if we get stuck in one of the valleys between them. That's where the rivers flow so it's easy to be drowned in our own sorrows.

Cougar broke into my thoughts. "But if you change your mind, eh?" He seemed relieved that I had not agreed to his suggestion. "But don't take too long. I am ready to share my life with a woman." He looked up toward the back of The Bear—we had reached its leg and were standing there beside its toes. "If I live long enough." He laughed a little bit as he lifted the coil of heavy rope off his shoulder. "What I will do is go up first and tie this to that big tree up there. Like last time. And you will wait here." He tied the rope around his waist. "As I climb you will feed the rope. Understand?"

I nodded. "Are you sure this will work? What if it gets caught on something?"

His smile told me to be quiet. "That's why I need you down here. To make sure that doesn't happen. I can't risk falling on top of you. I have to go alone."

"Be careful."

Like a squirrel up a tree, Cougar clambered up the leg of The Bear and was at the spot where the chipped-in foot and hand holds ended when he stopped and turned back to look at me. "This is where I fell."

"I slipped there, too. Don't look at it!"

"I want to."

"Don't."

But he did. "Ah."

"Don't do that, Cougar. Stop looking. Keep going."

"Doesn't look as bad as I remember. I think it was the shock of seeing it in the first place… Maybe. It's very sad, isn't it?"

"Yes. Keep going. Please."

"Na to'q, na to'q, all right, all right." He continued up the leg of The Bear but more slowly as there were no more foot and hand holds chipped into the rock and he had to pull himself up with branches and roots. It took a while and when he got to the top he waved down at me with a big smile. "Made it." I think he was trying to be reassuring and funny, but it didn't work.

It was now my turn to make my way up there—and back down again. I threw the rope around my waist and began to tie a secure knot.

"Wait a minute," he said. "Somebody's been here since we were."

"App? What did you say?"

"I said, somebody's been here since—"

"Yeah, yeah. Somebody. Who somebody? What do you see?"

"There are ropes up here. They weren't here last time. And they weren't hidden under the snow either, they're dry. Wait." And he disappeared from my sight.

"Where did you go? What are you doing?"

He reappeared over the spot where the piece of decoration was and yelled down at me. "I'm here and the cloth is gone. Can you see the rope leading down to that ledge there?"

He pointed at it and I could see it now. "Yes."

"Somebody came and got it."

"You sure?"

"It's not here anymore and it was too big for a bird to take for its nest. Too much human smell for an animal to want. If one could get up here."

"Did the one who killed the Father come and get it?" But Cougar had disappeared from the edge of The Bear's back so hadn't heard me.

He appeared above me again and started down.

"Loop the end of the rope around that tree and..." I struggled to get the knot out at my waist. "Use it to get down. I'll hold the rope and guide it, too, from down here."

With the rope looped around the tree, one end of it tied around his own waist and the other coiled around his forearm and feeding through as he descended, Cougar worked his way down but he had no sooner landed at the toes of The Bear when Gi'gwesu came running up to us.

"How did you find me?" I asked him, frowning, thinking he might have been following me around again like he did when he was very young. "You and the rest of the people in the village need to learn to mind their business."

"Everybody knows where you went." He was out of breath so leaned over onto his knees. "Marguerite told me to get you. The baby's sick."

"What baby?"

"Your baby. Well, it's Claude and Marguerite's baby now, or will be soon. But that doesn't matter. Come on."

The mother of One-Eyed Joe's idea about taking my mind off things wasn't working out very well for me. I should have gone onto the land, away from everybody, taken my chances with the sadness on my own.

"Père Gaëtan wants to baptize it right away. In case it dies, you know." He ignored my gasp of horror. "He wants to make sure it gets to his Heaven. Least that's what he said. Claude agrees with him."

"But Marguerite does not. Is that what you're saying?"

"E'e. She said she didn't go to all that trouble and expense getting a christening party organized for nothing. She wants to wait. She also said some stuff about Père Gaëtan's magic but she made me promise not to repeat it to you." Then Gi'gwesu grabbed me by the arm and tried to pull me along with him. "Come on. Let's go. She needs you to vote on her side."

Cougar was coiling the rope around his arm and gave me a head signal that said *Go*.

☽ ○ ☾

The baby was in the wikuom of Second Son and Apalqaqamej and it was trying to cry but it couldn't breathe right.

"I'm sorry, I'm sorry," said Apalqaqamej, her face all pale and sweaty from the fire in their wikuom. Second Son and three other men were busy changing the bark for skins on the outside of the structure even though it was almost summer and by midday it would be hot outside. "My man is trying to keep it warm in here for her. I'm sorry, Keskoua. I don't know what happened. My boy doesn't have the sickness."

From behind me, Marguerite's voice flew past my ear. "The baby is already hot. Look at the redness of her face. And you are trying to make her hotter? You fools! Give her to me!" And Marguerite brushed past me in that small space, nearly knocking me over, to grab the baby up and she went hustling out.

Apalqaqamej was too shocked to react except for the widening of her eyes, but I turned quickly and ran after Marguerite expecting she would be going to her house.

As I came out of the wikuom of Second Son and Apalqaqamej, I nearly knocked Second Son over as he was reaching up to put a skin up high above the entrance hole.

"Watch it!"

One of the men behind the wikuom, so was unable to see, called out "I'm doing the best I can."

"Not you," said Second Son. "The Frenchman's crazy woman. I'm happy to see that I am not the only one who has one."

"Hey," answered the man. "You thought you were specially chosen like those friends of Jesus or something?"

The other men laughed.

"Which way did she go," I demanded.

Dancing Raven stuck his head out from around the back of the wikuom and pointed toward the fort. "That way." And his eyes went up and down my body. "But here's a crazy one I wouldn't mind having for myself."

Second Son stepped away from the wikuom to admire his work, looked over at me and told Raven, "No. This one is truly crazy. She doesn't listen to anybody but the voices in her own head."

One of the others made a return comment drawing laughter from all of them but I didn't hear it as I was already on the run toward the fort, following Marguerite and the baby. From the corner of my eye I saw Gi'gwesu help the mother of One-Eyed Joe up from her cross-legged position at her cooking fire. She was looking tired and weak but had a look of great concern on her face as she watched Marguerite disappear down the path with the baby. Gi'gwesu replaced a heavy blanket around her shoulders then began waving and pointing at me.

I caught up to Marguerite at the fort where she asked for Monsieur St-Amand but he was attending to a soldier who had cut his thumb nearly off trying to insert a dagger into a musket barrel as a bayonet. We had to sit and wait. I was almost sick with worry. Then Gi'gwesu arrived with the mother of One-Eyed Joe who was almost falling down with lack of breath.

"She said her chest hurts today," Gi'gwesu told us as he helped the mother of One-Eyed Joe sit on the bench beside us. He adjusted her blanket again. "Inside. Like she ate something bad or something."

"Just a little bit," said the mother of One-Eyed Joe. "I am out of breath. That is what bothers me most. What is going on here? The boy tells me… the baby is sick."

"It can't breathe," I said. "Look at it. Listen to it."

"The old and the young," said the mother of One-Eyed Joe, her breath coming in short gasps as well and her failed attempt at a smile making me worry about her a lot, too.

"It's not an *it*, ma chérie, it's a she," Marguerite said to me as she switched the baby from one arm to the other. "Mon p'tit, she's gained weight since her birth. Why don't you hold her while we wait?"

The baby couldn't possibly be as heavy as Marguerite was making it out to be. I turned my face away because I knew what Marguerite was trying to do. "Why are we here? Grandmother knows how to take care of these sicknesses."

Marguerite had stood up and she was now standing right in front of me. "Here." And she thrust the wee thing at me, the skins around it flapping as she did so. "She needs to be re-bundled. She's coming apart. Can't you see?"

I turned my face the other way.

"Do it." And she placed the infant on my lap and stepped back. I had no choice but to reach out and catch my daughter before she rolled off onto the ground.

Two hands appeared at my knees and would have been there to catch the baby if I had not managed to do so.

"Père Gaëtan," I said. "Na to'q. I've got her. I won't let her fall." I knew what he was there for so I busied myself re-wrapping the skins around her tiny body while he talked to Marguerite and the mother of One-Eyed Joe. The baby was so tiny I found it hard to believe she was human, one of us, had come out of me, and she looked like Gi'gwesu.

A commotion arose over at the far side of the enclosure when three men came out of a door there. Two of the men were supporting another between them and this one was singing very loudly about a naked woman and a snake and the other men were laughing. The one in the middle appeared to be very drunk but when I saw the white cloth around his hand, I knew this must be the man who had hurt his thumb trying to take the knife attachment out of his musket. I felt bad for him because sometimes our people get hurt trying to create new tools, too. Right behind them came a man I knew had to be Monsieur St-Amand. Although I had heard a lot about him, I had never seen him. He was fair and quite handsome even by my people's standards and he had an air of authority about him. You could see he was a man used to giving orders that nobody dared to say no to. Not even me.

As soon as he saw us, he said something to the three men and the two sober ones stopped laughing right away and looked over at us. One of them put his hand over the mouth of the injured one and they led him away through another door. This I knew was the entrance to the soldiers' quarters even though I had never been there.

"A young one," said Monsieur St-Amand. His frown was serious but at the same time made me feel confidence in him. "Very young. Very small. Are you the mother?"

"Uh."

"Well?" This he said in a loud voice that made me almost drop her. "Are you?"

"E'e." And I held her up to him.

"Well then, open up those skins and let me listen to her."

I did as I was told and was surprised when he lifted her up to his ear. "Aha." And he handed her back to me and rushed away to the door at the far end of the enclosure.

"We must baptize her immediately," said Père Gaëtan. For the first time I noticed that he was wearing a different scarf than he usually wore and he was holding a small vial of water in his hand along with a tiny metal case. He pulled a small book from behind his wide cloth belt. "We will perform *Extrema unctio*, the last rites."

"No we will not," Marguerite interrupted. "We will not." She stood again and although she was not as tall as I, she seemed to tower over Père

Gaëtan. "I have explained things to you."

"Your husband wishes it done and I will comply with his wishes, madame."

"Ah, but you forget, Père, he is not yet my husband. Is he?" With a grand gesture and sweep of her arm, finger pointing at me, she said: "He is *her* husband. We have not yet received the annulment. Have we?"

Père Gaëtan didn't actually say it out loud but I saw his lips form the word *merde* and he stepped away from the baby and me. "Well, Keskoua? What have you to say about the soul of your daughter? Do you want it saved or not?"

I was thinking that since the baby was half White perhaps the White man's magic would work best on it to save it from whatever Père Gaëtan was telling me it needed saving from but something didn't seem right. "What does it need saving from?" I asked him.

"She," said Marguerite. "What does *she* need saving from?"

"E'e. She's right. What does this baby need saving from anyway? Does your god send little ones like this to be put on fire in that awful place that goes forever and ever."

"No, no, no. The Lord is loving and kind. He—"

"I don't like him at all. I lifted the baby off my lap and squeezed her close to my chest. Go away with your magic."

Just then, Monsieur St-Amand returned with several small glass vials with liquid in them. "Grandmother there taught me about many of your medicines and I have made potions from them. I keep these on hand all the time—they're fresh, don't worry" he assured me "for your people if they need them. And for our men, too." He handed them over to Marguerite then squatted beside me. "I have diluted the strength considerably because of her size. A wee thing like this," and he caressed her back with such loving kindness that it felt as though her healing had already begun, "can't take the same dosage as a fully grown man, now can she?" He smiled. "You're nursing her how many times a day now?"

I shook my head and the shame I felt for having abandoned her made my face turn hot. Beside me, the mother of One-Eyed Joe wheezed loudly enough to make all of us turn toward her.

"I see." Monsieur St-Amand rose and pulled a glass pipe out of his pocket. "This is a special pipe," he said to Marguerite. "Holding the bowl like this," and he demonstrated, "insert the stem into the child's mouth taking great care to point it into the pouch of the cheek." He stepped close to me again and did something to the baby that I couldn't see from my angle. "Like this."

Everybody said "Ah."

"This way, you don't risk sending the medicine… and I will give the child a dosage now… open one of the vials, please. … into the lungs."

Marguerite handed all but one of the vials to Gi'gwesu. "Don't drop any."

I had never seen my brother looking so serious. "Don't worry, I won't." And he leaned in like everybody else did, except me who was holding the baby and could only see from the side of my eye what Monsieur St-Amand was doing.

"There. That's how it's done. And she will move her tongue around and swallow that."

Everybody said "Ah."

"Six times a day before she nurses. Space out the time so she gets regular doses throughout the day. Understood?"

Everybody said "E'e, yes."

"And now, Grandmother, I will prepare a potion for you to take home with you. Same instructions but you will take water after you take the medicine. I will be only a minute and when I get back, I want everyone gone. Get that child back to whomever is looking after her and keep her warm! And I want to see her in three days. And you, too, Grandmother."

That night I dreamed again about being on the back of The Bear and throwing off the baby and the Father. But this time, Falcon and Claude were not with me. A woman was behind me. I could feel her and see little bits of her when I started to turn my head. But every time I turned around, she had moved to behind me again. I knew who she was but couldn't think of it. And all the while, at the bottom of The Bear, down below where the piece of decoration had been, and where the Father's brains had splashed, was Paul Le Putois yelling up at me that he would catch the baby. The baby was in the air and was falling so slowly she seemed to be flying and Paul Le Putois's arms were out and I knew he would catch her but once again, I woke up before he did.

Twenty-one

Word went around really fast that a baby and a Grandmother were both sick so several young men from the villages around had a big meeting in the clearing near The Bear. Claude, Mathieu, Cougar and the Lnu Saqamaw went to see them to try to settle them down but when young men get certain ideas into their heads that will make them think they will be doing something important—and especially if they agree with each other—you can't stop them with your words.

I got some of the story of everything that happened from Cougar. Claude got a big part of it from Monsieur St-Amand who was at the fort the whole time. The rest of it I got from one of the boys involved. (I think he was the one who might have started it.) At first I thought he was making himself out to be really important by meeting at The Bear because of his name, Singing Bear Cub, but when I got to know him, I knew he was sincere but fourvoyé, misguided (another good word I had learned from Geneviève).

Père Gaëtan heard about the meeting and started over to see what he could do but Dancing Raven stopped him near the entrance to the clearing. "Some of these boys have a deep hatred for priests and I don't blame them, but you're a good man, Père, so I don't want to see you die. Go away."

Père Gaëtan came to me all concerned, then, about what might happen and I told him he was better to stay in his house for the next little while.

"I will pray in the church."

"I advise against it." I almost laughed at myself for saying this. I was sounding like Claude, like Monsieur St-Amand, even like Père Gaëtan himself by saying something like *I advise against it.* Was I already turning into a Grandmother giving advice out to people even though I was still very young?

The way Père Gaëtan looked at me told me he was surprised, too. "Do you know something I do not?"

"These young men are angry with everything to do with White ways right now, especially with White man's magic—"

Père Gaëtan opened his mouth to say something but I kept talking.

Wasn't I turning into a confident woman not to let a man interrupt me with his own opinions against what I was saying? I had to smile inside at myself again. "The magic of Monsieur St-Amand and… I'm sorry to say it, Père Gaëtan, but your magic, too."

Oncc again Père Gaëtan wanted to say something.

"They hear stories from the Grandfathers—and their own fathers. Visitors come with their stories of what has happened to them and *their* people. These boys are old enough now to have their own visions of what their life will be. They've gone onto the land alone so they are no longer children. I think maybe your church will be a target of their…" I had to look around in my head for the right word: "… misunderstandings."

"Misunderstandings?" Père Gaëtan turned away slightly and put his hand over his forehead to press his thumb and fingers into his temples. "Misunderstanding? They are preparing to sack and burn and perhaps kill over a misunderstanding?"

I nodded.

"And what, pray tell, is this misunderstanding they are suffering under?"

"The main one is the sickness they think is going through our village. They are saying all of us will die unless they kill Monsieur St-Amand to make him stop using his bad magic on us."

What came out of Père Gaëtan made him sound like a startled cougar. "Aaagh. Bad magic? Magic? It's medicine he gives. He would not harm anyone."

"I know that. And the medicine he gave to the mother of One-Eyed Joe was her own. He just put something extra in to make it easier for the baby to drink and to make it not go bad."

"Fools. They're all fools." He pinched his temples again.

"They're young. They want to protect their community. They are learning how to be men."

"Learn? Who will be here to teach them if they kill the doctor—and me? Who else do they wish to destroy? The soldiers? Who will teach them right from wrong if they kill all of *us*?"

I didn't think this was funny. It was sad that Père Gaëtan seemed on the outside to be willing to learn our ways and to respect us and our ideas, but on the inside he was the same as the other priests after all. I guess sometimes you have to peel off the bark to see if the worms have gotten into the tree or not. I turned away. "Maybe if you pray to your god he might stop those young men from hurting... 'you people.'" I didn't wait for a response but went to see what I could find out about the plans of the young men. I didn't find out anything that day but I saw Claude, Mathieu, Cougar, Dancing Raven and the Lnu Saqamaw coming back to the village just after the sun went away and just before the drums and songs of the young men started up.

Claude saw me and stopped at my wikuom. "I want you to come with me. We'll collect Marguerite and Chipmunk and the baby. You ladies will stay in the fort."

"That's the last place we should be," I said. "Because that's the first place they will go. They need to get rid of the soldiers. Only then can they do what they want, where they want." Well. Wasn't I turning into a wise woman lately? "Bring Marguerite here. I'll hide her for you."

But he brought her to the fort instead. Apalqaqamej wouldn't go with them.

☽ ○ ☾

Nothing happened until the next morning when Singing Bear Cub, followed by about twenty young men carrying all manner of weapons and running on silent feet, went through our village on the way to the fort. They had bows and arrows and spears and knives and some of them carried muskets and powder bags. If the situation hadn't been so serious I would have been laughing and pointing at them. There they were, wanting to fight the ways of the White people but using the White people's tools, like metal knives and guns, to do it with.

Before long, I heard far-off noises like dead trees falling on rocks but knew it was musket shots. Then silence. A few more cracks and two men yelling. I didn't recognize the language or their voices as it was just a cry of surprise and pain. Before long, all the men—as far as I could count anyway—came back. Singing Bear Cub was being helped along because he had been injured, probably shot, but not in the heart to kill him, but in the leg. I could see some blood there. This showed me that the men at the fort did not want to kill these young men, only show they could if they wanted to.

Singing Bear Cub asked his friends to stop so he could talk to the mother of One-Eyed Joe but I stepped in front of him and asked him what he wanted with her. One of the boys supporting him held a musket in his other hand and kept turning the front of his body to me whenever I moved. Behind him, two Grandmothers looked over and started to laugh.

"She can heal my wound," said Singing Bear Cub pointing to the blood on his leg.

I looked down at it and saw that it was something that Monsieur St-Amand called a flesh wound and that it was black with powder.

"Monsieur Hermel St-Amand at the fort can heal you, too. He uses Grandmother's medicine on our people. Did you know that?"

Singing Bear Cub and his three companions all looked at each other and two of them put their heads down as if they were ashamed. Singing Bear Cub didn't put his head down but he wouldn't look me in the eye, either. Behind the boy with the musket, several young ones ran past with their hands over their mouths laughing.

"Monsieur St-Amand is a good man. He gave my baby some of the medicine he learned from the mother of One-Eyed Joe and my baby is doing better. Go see it. I mean her. Go see her. She is in the wikuom of Second Son over there." I pointed.

"Is this true?" asked Singing Bear Cub and his companions moved closer to me to hear what I might say.

"Of course it's true. Why would I tell you an untruth? Who are you to me?"

"Can you heal my leg?"

I motioned him to enter my wikuom. "I learned many things from the mother of One-Eyed Joe. I'll see what I can do to fix your wound. Eh. It's on the back of your leg. How did it happen? I don't think a soldier would shoot you if you were going away from him. Would he?"

As he bent down to go through the entranceway to my wikuom he made a motion with his head toward the boy holding the musket. Once inside he whispered to me "That idiot with the gun. He never used one before, eh. He loaded it the way he has watched others do it many times but he put too much powder in and was trying to get some of it back out so was sitting down by a tree and holding it across himself when the other idiot told him he could just burn it out if he lit the fuse. He did. The musket ball got me in the leg and the powder set fire to the front of his loin cloth. He had to turn it around. You see that?"

I could hear the laughter of more children outside my wikuom. I wondered how long it would take for the young man to recover from that shame.

"When you are done with me, he will want you to look under his loin cloth."

"I will do so," I assured him. "Let's have a look at that leg of yours."

What could have been a terrible thing between our people and the soldiers ended up being an exchange of opinions with nobody getting really hurt. Singing Bear Cub's wound was not serious so it was easy for him to look after himself using the plants I gave him. The burn under the young man's loin cloth was not severe either but it hurt and I knew it would end up hurting even more over the next few days when the nerves started to grow back. For an extra lesson, I told him I had none of the special ointment left and he would have to go ask Monsieur St-Amand at the fort. At first he refused but after only one day of agony, the young man changed his mind.

Twenty-two

Some of our people lived for a long, long time but the mother of One-Eyed Joe wasn't one of them. She got over her sickness but because she was an old woman, she was too weak to keep going.

Monsieur St-Amand said it was her heart that was giving out and that we should let her rest and be quiet and not to have so many people always going in there and talking to her all the time.

"She needs rest. Let the woman rest, pour l'amour de Dieu!" He liked her a lot because she had helped him many times with not only our people but with the soldiers, too. I heard she had once cured Monsieur St-Amand himself of something but I never heard what it was. I think it was something embarrassing.

We knew he was getting more and more worried about her because we would find him walking back and forth near her wikuom every morning before the sun came up.

One day there was a line of about twenty people waiting to see her and he yelled out very loud and angrily. "Stay away from her! Must I post a guard?"

Three of our men stepped forward toward him and touched the

handles of the knives that were in their belts. They said nothing but they didn't need to.

Somebody ran to get the Lnu Saqamaw and he came up to them and told our men to be calm, that he would explain things, and he took Monsieur St-Amand away to the clearing near The Bear. When they returned, Monsieur St-Amand went into the mother of One-Eyed Joe's wikuom himself for a brief moment and when he came back out he was smiling and happy.

My turn came soon enough.

"Greetings, Grandmother," I said and I handed her my tobacco offering in its little pouch. I saw that she had a big pile of these in one corner of the wikuom. "I wish you a good Journey."

"Thank you, Granddaughter. What is it you wish to speak to me about?"

She was burning special wood that did not give off much smoke and I sat across the small flame from her. I began to speak and told her of the many times she had helped me and how valuable her life had been to have her in mine. I ended with: "And I am sorry for all the times I got mad at you for getting mad at me." I hung my head down because I knew that if I kept looking into her eyes, mine would fill with water and that would make her sad. She could not be sad now. It was important for her to be happy before she left on her Journey."

"I forgive you, Granddaughter. How is Jeanne? Your child?"

I was surprised she would say this to me. Was she trying to make me cry? Was she putting me to a test? To see how strong I had become since I was a child myself?

"She is well now. She has recovered from her sickness."

She was used to my silences as well as my outbursts.

"I did not get my sickness from her if it will make you feel any better. Maybe she got it from me, eh?" and she laughed which made me smile at her and look into her eyes after all. Her eyes were happy. "My sickness is because I am over sixty winters old. My own mother did not live past fifty winters so my ancestors have been waiting extra long for me to arrive. It's time for me to go and see what I can do to help people out, eh?" And she smiled again.

"You always make me feel good, Grandmother."

She patted my knee. "Go now, Granddaughter. Send the next one in. I am happy that many people are wishing me well on my Journey. It means I have lived a good life, e'e?"

When everyone in our village and those from the fort and from Falcon's village, too, had been to visit her, even the little ones, we started the line over again to see her. We had all seen her two times and about half of us three when One-Eyed Joe came to me and said "She wants to see us. You, me and Young Rabbit Woman. It's time for her to leave on her Journey."

I knew I would miss her. We all would miss her. But we were all happy that she would be going on her Journey and that she would be able to help us in our dreams now whenever we asked. I think she was even happier about this. We entered the wikuom and outside, everyone gathered and the men began to drum and sing happy songs and the people danced and laughed until we came out of the wikuom just before the sun went away.

"She's on her way and she told us she will have an easy passage," said One-Eyed Joe and beside him, Young Rabbit Woman and I grabbed each other and let out all the tears we had been holding in since the mother of One-Eyed Joe had taken sick.

Everyone joined us in our crying, even the men.

The beat of the drums changed and so did the songs as the others went their own way to help prepare for the burial ceremony. Many of the women had already been preparing for the burial feast that would follow the ceremony so a lot of the preparations were already done.

As they were leaving, one of the young boys said in a choked voice "But I don't want to cry, Mother. It's not manly."

One-Eyed Joe went to the boy and put his hand on his shoulder. "E'e, it *is* manly, my boy. It takes a strong man to show his true feelings to others."

Young Rabbit Woman and I went back into the wikuom to collect the belongings of the mother of One-Eyed Joe and these we wrapped in skins and piled on a travois that we would be bringing to the burial site.

My mother entered the wikuom with an armful of skins and she began to prepare the body to be wrapped. "The men are preparing the carrying poles," was all she said.

Claude, Mathieu, Cougar and a couple of other men went to prepare the burial mound and Young Rabbit Woman and I dragged the travois with all the belongings of Grandmother to where they were.

The burial hole was deep and it nestled close to a tamarack tree. I knew she would be pleased with everything about it.

It was not long before the men with the bundle of skins on the carrying pole arrived and Grandmother was placed in her new home and we put her belongings in with her. We hung special symbols on sticks beside it then the Lnu Saqamaw said a few words and so did Monsieur Hermel St-Amand and Père Gaëtan.

At first the feast was quiet but even before everyone had eaten their fill, the drums and the singing and the dancing started and all of us—even Père Gaëtan—joined to honor Grandmother's Journey and her new name: Natawinpiteget, Good Healer.

Twenty-three

I had hoped that the marriage ceremony for Claude and Marguerite (which Père Gaëtan had insisted be combined with the baptism of little Jeanne, my baby) would take my mind off everything that had been going on and was still going on—Falcon was still missing, for one, and my people had just buried the mother of One-Eyed Joe—but it didn't. The Mass for the mother of One-Eyed Joe had not been any different than usual, either, and had only made me think of everything bad that had been happening to everybody lately. The only good thing about this marriage ceremony Mass for Claude and Marguerite was that when Père Gaëtan gave the talk in the middle, he wasn't as angry as he usually was—but he didn't shorten it any.

He ended it by saying "And may you have many children."

Most of our people didn't go to the Masses so weren't expecting this from a priest so they laughed because for us this always meant "may you have fun on the kaksk'ug until you die of old age." But because this seemed to make the faces of Marguerite's relatives turn serious as if it would be a terrible chore, I looked down at my hands and remembered how the Father had put the baby in my belly. Maybe that's how the French had to make babies happen. Maybe that's how our people had to make babies happen, too, but why did our people always say it was wonderful and pleasurable then? I would have to ask Claude about that—or maybe it would be better to ask Marguerite now that Claude was a married man and not to me anymore.

The feast after the wedding ceremony was not at all like ours. Geneviève would have used the word "merveilleux." We all went to Claude's barn because there was enough room for everyone there. Claude and several men had moved the stalls and Gesm'pisit over to Mathieu's new barn for a few days. Yes, Claude had agreed with me that he would keep Gesm'pisit from being made into sausages like he had saved her mother, l'Orignal-Sale—and her daughters would be safe from the frying pan, as well. The men had cleaned Claude's barn all up and hung kaksk'us on the walls to try to cover up the smell of pig. The candles with their special perfumes helped, too.

But I must tell you about the music. It was amazingly loud and seemed to turn everyone—me, too—into a frenzy of moving feet and dancing. I was used to moving my feet a certain way so it took me a few tries to get it right, but once I did, I liked it a lot. People took turns singing and for the faster songs, people took turns dancing alone, too, up there in front of everybody with all the people clapping along and tapping their own feet. Great cheers went up whenever anybody finished their own dance and another person took over. Some of the little kids were better than the adults. Like our people, they mostly moved just their feet but they moved them a lot faster. There were no drums like ours but Marguerite's sister sat on a chair beside the other musicians and banged two backwards spoons together between one knee and her cupped hand in a fast rhythm while Marguerite's father used a metal rod to bang on a triangle, also of metal.

"That triangle mon oncle is using? Ceci s'appelle *un 'tit-fer*," explained the woman standing to my right, a cousin of Marguerite, "a little bit of iron. My grandfather—Marguerite's grandfather, too—taught him to play it."

They made a nice sound together and I was surprised at the different sounds the 'tit-fer could make depending on where Monsieur Petitpas struck it and whether on the inside or the outside of it, or how hard. Monsieur Petitpas knew a soldier from the fort who played what they called a fiddle: a beautiful shiny red-painted box with a womanly waist and strings from what would be her chin to where her legs would meet. He scraped a stick across this box to make sounds like a woman inside it was singing the highest notes possible. It made bumps on my skin to hear it. Later I saw that the stick had many fine threads from one end of it to another. Marguerite's cousin—her name was Antoinette—told me the threads were made of catgut but that the catgut was sheep guts. (I would never understand these people.)

Our people had many different dances: the jingle dance and the shawl dance were for women and the fancy dance was for both men and women but not together. The hoop dance was for anyone who could do it. When I was small I thought I'd like to learn the hoop dance and I got to be good at it up to fourteen hoops, but after that I wasn't very good. I could do the dance and fit the hoops together like they were supposed to go but after fourteen hoops I would be paying so much attention to getting them to where they were supposed to be and keep my feet moving right, too, that I would forget to listen for the end of the song and wouldn't stop when the song stopped. I was never as good as I had wanted to be, but I was good enough at doing it to show our little ones how. I heard that one time Falcon got up to thirty-two hoops before he tripped and fell over. Nobody laughed at him for that because nobody else had ever been able to get past twenty-eight. For our round dances, everybody could join in, men, women and children and even babies in their mothers' arms, and we would move around in a circle sideways around the drummers in the middle. The songs would get faster and faster and we would have to move along with the music and keep step and try not to laugh because it was hard enough work to keep that pace for so many songs.

Antoinette told me that the French had a contredanse, and a cotillion, and a quadrille and Marguerite was at the same time calling out the names of these dances from the middle of everybody as she and Claude danced in each of them. "*Explain this one to her,*" Marguerite cried out one time to Antoinette about me over the music.

"*I am. Don't worry about her. Just have fun.* This will be the last fun you'll have for the rest of your life. You should know that." And she patted her own belly and this was when I noticed that she would be having a baby very soon.

"Don't have that baby tonight, eh?" I said to her and laughed.

And this made her laugh so hard she rushed away outside. I knew I had made her start to lose her water. When she came back I asked if she was all right.

"I made it in time this time," she said to me, still with a big smile on her face. I liked her.

I was surprised when Mathieu got up near the people who were making the music and made them all stop so people could hear him. Everybody went really quiet and I wondered what went wrong. I was just about to ask Antoinette if she had heard anything when she was outside, when Mathieu spoke.

"Who wants these fellows to play une danse carrée, a square dance?"

Everyone cheered and they got into groups of eight, two-by-two facing across from each other in a square, then the music started up again loud and fast and everybody grabbed arms and swung around and changed partners and went under each other's arms and crossed over from side to side. I didn't know how they could remember to do the same steps together this fast and so well until I realized that Mathieu was calling out instructions.

À l'main gauche, de l'main gauche

Retournez l'dame à l'homme à l'droite
Traversez à l'avant à l'arrière
Retournez l'dame à son Pierre…

Next thing I knew, Marguerite was at my side, laughing and breathing hard and I was in Claude's arms up on the dance floor being passed to the man beside me and swung around back to Claude. It was great fun until a loud bang at the barn doors caused the music to die out and everybody to stop and turn around to see what had happened.

"Merde," said Antoinette from behind me. "Giacomo l'Italien and Little Cock are at it again."

Little Cock was lying on the floor with his head against the big barn door—that's what had made the bang—when I turned. But no matter how drunk he ever got, he was still quick on his feet so was up and swinging at Giacomo l'Italien—we called him Jacques l'Itale—almost instantly. "You ruined my daughter, you God-cursed foreigner."

Both Marguerite and her cousin laughed behind their hands.

"I heard he did it himself," whispered Marguerite past me to Antoinette. "Got drunk and thought he was with his mother."

Both women burst into laughter that they tried to keep others from hearing.

Antoinette said: "No. That's only in the North that happens."

"What a terrible thing to say." Marguerite didn't mean this at all as she was still laughing and making Antoinette clutch her belly to stop it from bouncing along with her. "They only do it with each other's wives up there."

A couple of other women near us had heard their comments and one of them said: "Or with each other." And all of us laughed.

In the background, Jacques l'Itale and Little Cock were calling each other names and trying to hit each other without falling over. They were both very drunk so were having trouble staying upright. One would fall and the other would help him up then take a swing at him which would make himself fall. As this went on, everybody was watching and laughing but from the side of my eye I saw—or maybe I felt—Antoinette suddenly twitch and her left hand shot out to grasp my elbow.

"Merde," she said and looked down at her feet where a puddle of liquid was expanding into its own lake. "Merde."

I pulled at Marguerite's sleeve, pointed to the floor at Antoinette's feet, and she turned and said merde, too. "I'll get her husband." And off she floated toward Claude and the two men who were standing and laughing with him.

The woman in front of me spoke to the one beside her. "I can't believe Marguerite invited these riffraff. I could see her new 'husband' doing it, but—"

Mathieu, whom I had not noticed behind me, spoke up. "They came in the hopes of stealing brandy." He moved up to fill the spot to my left that Marguerite had vacated.

A man hurried over to Antoinette's side and took her arm and with his and Marguerite's help, Antoinette managed to waddle away toward the back of the barn and the big wooden doors there. Someone had already backed a travois into it and hitched up a cow.

The woman in front of me turned. "How could you possibly know that, monsieur. You were up there yelling directions for that abomination you people call la danse carrée."

A young man scurried in with cloths to wipe up the water that Antoinette's baby had spilled on the floor.

Mathieu winked at me before raising his own nose as high as madame's. He replied: "I know that because they do that all the time, Ta Majesté."

I bit my lip so I wouldn't smile. I liked him, too.

He continued. "Whenever there is a gathering, whenever people are distracted by dancing and singing and enjoying themselves, these two men sneak in and try to steal something to keep that fire of theirs burning. Both the fire of alcohol and the fire of fight." He leaned in close to her and whispered loudly enough for me and everyone else close by to hear: "I can confide that they are a constant canker on the poxied arse of the innkeeper."

My hand moved instantly to cover my mouth in the hopes that my giggle would not escape but I wasn't fast enough.

The woman made a sound like a Gesm'pisit makes when she gets a bit of dust in her nose and marched away after Antoinette's entourage.

The fight between Jacques l'Itale and Little Cock had moved outside as had half of the guests. I didn't plan to miss anything either so with Mathieu leading the way, I worked myself through the remaining crowd to stand outside. But before anything else could happen, Père Gaëtan intervened and pulled Jacques l'Itale aside.

I had ended up standing beside Claude and Marguerite and we were all close enough to hear that Père Gaëtan was saying something about the "traditions of the Native people" and "Native girls are not like your Italian girls, Giacomo. The tradition is that a Native girl remains a virgin until marriage."

"Tabernacle—" Claude began.

"Claude. What have I told you about such lang—"

"Père Gaëtan," Claude continued. "No wonder I don't go to Mass and listen to you priests about what the 'Natives believe.' Only when you make a baby with a woman are you considered married here. Get it straight." Claude patted Père Gaëtan on the back. "I like you, you know. Sometimes you even make sense. Sometimes." Claude laughed and Père Gaëtan slid his arm around Claude's back and Claude reciprocated with his arm over the other man's shoulder. "But, oh mon Dieu, tabernacle.

You can be très stupid sometimes."

It took three men to get the protesting Little Cock away from the crowd that was already thinning as people were lighting lanterns and heading for home. "I'll get you for this, t'maudit étranger. I'll get all of you damné coureurs de bois, hostie. And I'll start with that crazy one. The son of that even crazier Scotsman. What's his name? You'll all thank me for this. What? You have a bottle of Scotch? Ah. Bless your heart. I love all you coureurs de bois. You are all such kind, generous people." And Little Cock's voice faded away into nothing but his threat did not.

☽ ○ ☾

Four of our people were missing from the feast following the wedding ceremony of Claude and Marguerite: Falcon, Geneviève and her son Paul Le Putois, and Feather—again.

I asked Cougar if he knew where Feather was and he said he hadn't seen her since before my baby was born. He thought maybe she was at the Moon Time wikuom.

"She's not there," I told him. I knew Geneviève wasn't there, either, for the same reason. I had sent two of the little girls to see.

I asked Young Rabbit Woman if she knew anything about where Geneviève was. I knew that Geneviève liked her and they often talked to each other so thought Young Rabbit Woman might have some idea of where she went. The most important thing I learned was that Geneviève had found out that the Father wasn't a Father a few days before he was killed. She was cleaning up his house and came across some papers hidden behind a drawer in a bureau. Geneviève told him she was going to tell everybody about him and who he really was, unless he did it first.

She thought he was very wrong, Young Rabbit Woman said, to pretend he was a priest and listen to people's Confessions and find out all about them and he hadn't taken the vow not to give their secrets away.

This made her very angry.

I wondered how many secrets Geneviève had told him in Confession. I wondered how many secrets Claude and Marguerite had told him and Monsieur St-Amand and Mathieu and all the others. Feather, too. Maybe Feather knew about this and this is why she had gone away.

"Does Feather know about this?"

She shrugged. "I don't know. I don't know who knows. I only know that Geneviève was very angry. But I also know the Father got so angry, he frightened Geneviève. She thought maybe he was wanting to kill her."

"I can't see the Father killing anybody. He was… He…"

"E'e. I know what you mean. He…"

"But it would have brought back bad memories for her, eh? It doesn't matter how weak a man is. If you are afraid of him, he has power over you."

"E'e."

Twenty-four

Around this time, Mathieu, who had been away delivering supplies—mostly liquor—to the loggers up on Crête des Pins, came running into the village with word that the men there had been seeing a woman wandering through the bush there. "But she was… How do I say?" Mathieu asked, shrugging. "Très insaisissable. So they think she's a ghost."

"All women are elusive—intangible—my friend. Especially for you," said Claude, laughing and teasing his friend. "Oh, Mathieu, mon ami. Have you had so much success with only old women lately that you are turning into one yourself with your gossip?"

One-Eyed Joe and several other people who had gathered around laughed. Mathieu did not. I heard he was spending a lot of time with one of Dancing Raven's older sisters, the one I could never remember the name of. She was quite pretty and very quiet and shy, so I wondered how Mathieu had ever convinced her to be with him.

"Some are saying it's the fantôme of that woman who bashed her husband's brains in," Mathieu continued, at first his eyes almost as big as Paul Le Putois's were when he and his mother moved away from there and back to our village. "Others say it's the actual woman. I think her name is

Geneviève, is it not? Yes. That's it. Geneviève. Lovely name mais une dame bizarre, n'est pas? Crazier than crazy. Either would not be something to exclude from the list of possibilities, but others are saying it was Our Blessed Mother, La Sainte Vierge, and I'm more inclined toward that direction myself. You know, like people are seeing in Saint-Étienne-le-Laus back home in France these last few years." As the crowd grew, Mathieu's voice got slightly louder. "There's no reason La Sainte wouldn't come here, too. Is there?" He leaned forward toward Père Gaëtan, spread his hands outward, and smiled. "That would be special, wouldn't it?" Then he turned to the others again, still with his supplicating hands held out. "We would become rich in no time." He had caught his breath already from the run but was getting excited with the idea that he had an audience, that people were listening to him talk of their Blessed Virgin, so he was breathing hard from that. He was a good talker so maybe this was how he managed to get the older sister of Dancing Raven interested in him. He was smart, too.

Like I said before, I was always amazed by some of these coureurs de bois. Some of them could run for hours. Not me. Not Claude either. And whenever I mentioned this to Claude, he always told me he had received brains from God, not legs and lungs, and that I should mind my own business and pay attention to whatever it was I happened to be doing at the time I mentioned it. One of the other things that amazed me—enough that I want to say it again—was the way they lived their lives cheating each other and everybody else, taking our women, and even killing each other, and still believed that by doing these very things that they would go to that place called Hell but it didn't stop them from doing them.

"Most likely a fantôme," said Charles who had followed Mathieu into the village and was sitting on the ground trying to recover his breath without much luck. "Lots of those up there. The Scotsman for one. They say… They say that on the anniversary of his death he will sometimes make a tree fall wrong so it lands on one of the men. Out of revenge, of course. Everybody knows it was the fault of the loggers he got his head bashed in in the first place."

"If it's Geneviève wandering around up there it's out of guilt," said Claude. "We haven't seen her for a very long time. Have we?" With his eyebrows up, he looked around at the group but nobody said anything. "Not since Father Soucy was killed." He turned to Charles: "And what The Scotsman got, he brought upon himself from what I understand."

A couple of people grunted agreement.

"The boy is a man now, you know. Have they seen him?" asked the Lnu Saqamaw.

"Paul Le Putois is what they call him," said Père Gaëtan as if nobody knew. "Never attends Mass. Never." He shook his head in the saddest manner.

I didn't think going to Mass would cure what had eaten Le Putois's brain from the inside. I didn't think anything would.

"No boy. No man. Seulement le fantôme, or whatever she is," Mathieu said. "What would she be doing back up there? She would not ever go back there after what she did..."

"The loggers are a very superstitious bunch," offered Père Gaëtan and he got a look from more than me for that one. He continued. "They are no doubt imagining this appearance out of guilt for their sins. Our Blessed Mother would never appear to such men. They refuse to attend daily Mass no matter how many priests we send to—"

"People have to pay for their sins," said Charles and this made One-Eyed Joe step forward toward him. Charles didn't move back—I would have and so would many others feeling what was coming out of One-Eyed Joe right then—but instead, he raised himself taller and stuck his big stomach out.

"This man Charles is not who he says he is. Is he?" I whispered to

Claude. "Who is he really?"

"I won't speak his name."

It seemed that Mathieu had not noticed this interaction between One-Eyed Joe and Charles. "It's not screams this time, they say. It's crying. Really sad broken-heart crying." Mathieu was "pontificating" now—another of the new words I'd learned from Geneviève and this reminded me of how important she was to us and made me worry about her even more if it was true that she was wandering around in the bush up near Crête des Pins. Several more people had arrived and were listening. Mathieu straightened his shoulders and adjusted his belt that had all manner of things hanging off it. I recognized the use for some of them. Others I did not want to guess in case I got my guess right. "If it is she, then she finally went over." He tapped his temple. "Elle est devenue folle comme un balai, she has gone crazy as a dust-mop." He shook his head. "And that is why I prefer to think it is a sign from God." He raised his eyes heavenward.

Mutterings of both approval and disapproval flowed through the group.

"And I know where that boy of Keskoua's got himself to as well," he added, really savoring the attention now. "Charles here told me."

"Dis-toi?" asked several people at once.

"I know where Falcon is. Le Putois has him. Up in the cabin at Mouse Ridge. Up there where he shot Jean-Baptiste Bourque in the back."

A ripple of oohs washed over all of us and a wave of weakness passed through my heart, chilling it. I glanced over at Charles whose face now had a strange look on it that could have been a smile but it wasn't.

Nobody said anything but they all went away in different directions except for me because I didn't know what was going on. Claude had almost disappeared down the path to his house when he stopped and came back.

"Go," he said. "Go visit your mother or your brother or somebody." And he turned me around and pushed me away from him. "You will have no part in this."

I turned back. "But I want to go with you. Maybe Falcon needs me—"

"What Falcon needs—" and he grasped my shoulders and he wasn't very gentle about it, either.

"Ow. That hurts. Don't—"

"What Falcon needs is for you to go visit your mother or your brother or somebody. Did you not hear me the first time?"

I pulled away from him and crossed my arms and was about to say more but there was something in his eyes that I had never seen before.

"If you have any love for me," he said slowly, "any at all, you will do as I ask."

I didn't say anything but I uncrossed my arms. I was getting really scared now. "Do you think—?"

He put one finger against my lips. "Shh. Please."

I nodded.

"Promise."

"I promise."

He ran off again down the path toward his place and I could hear the other men returning from where they had been, their voices low and grumbling like they were wolves and cougars planning to go hunting but didn't like the idea of doing it together.

I waited for several breaths before I ducked behind a tree to hide from them. Eight men entered the clearing, two of them with guns, three with bows, and three with the heels of their hands on the gutting knives in their belts.

"Where's La Verdure?" one of them asked. It was Charles. He was one of those with a gun. Little Cock was the other.

"We should wait," said Mathieu, but Charles had already started away.

Mathieu called out to their backs. "Well I'm going to wait for him."

This fell on deaf ears as the other men were already following Charles.

"Chalice." When Mathieu said this he turned slightly and caught sight of me behind the tree. I hadn't been fast enough to hide myself again. He repeated the curse then said my name in the most gentle way I have ever heard it spoken. "You cannot be a part of this. You must not know about any of this. Please. Go."

I went.

I got most of the story out of Falcon himself as he was with Paul Le Putois the whole time Le Putois was dying and talking, but other parts came from Claude and Mathieu and even from Charles, the one who gut-shot Le Putois.

Twenty-five

"The leg won't heal if you keep drinking," said Le Putois through the cabin door after he had shut and bolted it on the outside. "If you want to make Keskoua happy, you must stop with that nonsense. Since you don't have the courage to do it yourself I will do it for you. And I am a coward. What does that make you?"

This was the point where Falcon fully woke up in a state of absolute rage at being tricked into following Paul Le Putois out to Mouse Ridge to be trapped inside the cabin there. But he told me most of what followed was a blur of bugs, pain, shivering and throwing most of what he ate and drank—rice, boiled grouse, corn, bannock, water and potions—back up out of his stomach into buckets set here and there on the floor of the cabin.

This is what happened to Falcon and he told me this when we were sitting on chairs in a private room at the fort and had Monsieur St-Amand hovering over us like he was a sparrow protecting his nest from a crow. It seemed like Monsieur Hermel St-Amand liked Falcon a lot. Many of the soldiers at the fort liked our people even though they weren't supposed to "collaborate" with us. (Another word I learned from Geneviève.) The soldiers who had been posted at the settlement at Québec and had then been posted here afterwards, said there was a big difference between the Québec people and the people of l'Acadie. I heard some say—some of the soldiers who were old now and who had been all over the world—that there was nowhere else like l'Acadie and the people here and how everybody—for the most part—got along.

Falcon had been having one of his special naps, he said, so was pretty much passed out in his wikuom and leaning back against a supporting strut when a sound made him open his eyes and there was Paul Le Putois right up against his face asking him if he wanted to share a drink together and waggling a half-empty bottle up high in the air out of reach. Falcon was surprised for two reasons. One: Paul Le Putois hadn't touched alcohol for years, at least as far as Falcon knew; and two: Paul Le Putois had told Falcon only a few days earlier that he was in love with me and would prefer to see Falcon dead but wanted to see if he could do him one last favor first. At the time, this offer of a favor frightened Falcon because first of all, this was almost always the way the White people began the ruination of one of our people's lives, and second of all, it sounded like a threat. But after a bottle or two of brandy following that encounter, the fear—as well as the memory of it—had become unimportant. Besides, Paul Le Putois had never been known to attack anybody right up front if they knew it was coming. He liked to sneak up behind them and catch them when they were paying attention to something else. If they were still alive, you could have asked the Portugais (who ended up with a bullet hole in the back of his jacket and his bones gnawed by animals and scattered all over the bush), or Jean-Baptiste Bourque (who ended up with a bullet in his back, too), or Le Putois's own father (who ended up with his brains all over the place) about that.

The power of brandy over common sense has caused the death of a lot more men than Paul Le Putois ever killed—probably a lot more than anybody ever killed—and since Falcon was under the magic of brandy and since he had already finished his only bottle of drink that morning, and was also out of money, and was also now feeling pain not just in his head but everywhere, especially in his healing leg, he stretched up and snatched the bottle away from Paul and nearly emptied it without taking a breath.

"Whoa. Slow down. Slow down," said Paul, grabbing the bottle away from Falcon's lips. "I know where there's more. Let's go before you fall back to sleep, hein?"

"That tasted bad," said Falcon trying to spit. "Where did you get that from? Are you trying to poison me?" He reached for the bottle. "Let me see the label. What symbol is on it? Let me see who made it."

But Paul pulled the bottle out of range of Falcon's long arm and said "That's not important. Come on. We have to go. I know where there's a big supply of liquor." Taking Falcon's upper arm on his bad side, Paul tried to lift him up off the kaksk'ug. "A big supply. And nobody else knows about it."

"Tasted like shit," muttered Falcon as he easily got to a standing position with Paul's help. "Who made it? Must have been Indians? Squaws maybe, eh? To make us not like it anymore, hey? Hey, ha. E'e. That's it. That's it." And he laughed at his joke so hard he fell back down onto the kaksk'ug again.

Paul Le Putois was not a big man but he was strong so he managed to get Falcon back onto his feet and together they walked out of the village with Paul holding the bottle up high in the air on the side away from Falcon, and supporting Falcon, limping along, arm stretched across Paul's shoulder like they were the best of friends, on the other. This was how they left the village but nobody paid any attention. I have no blame to put into the dreams of those who never saw men like these leaving the village. I myself was guilty of always looking away in sorrow from men who were doing this, always hoping that maybe if I didn't see them, didn't see their shame, it would no longer be true.

It took a long time, Falcon said, to get to where they were going. Paul would not tell him no matter how much Falcon begged him to do so. And slowly, through his drunken fog, Falcon became aware that Paul probably knew enough to never tell somebody you didn't like that you were taking them to a place where you had shot somebody else you hadn't liked, in the back.

The journey was long, Falcon said, and there were parts he didn't remember. The thing he did remember most was that Paul kept saying "You have to keep moving. Keep moving. You can't slow down and you must not, for sure, lie down until I get you there. Come on. Help me. Keep moving."

Falcon said he was surprised that the pain in his leg had lessened so much after he had drunk the brandy Paul had given him. Part of his mind kept telling him that Paul had poisoned him with something that was making him want to sleep, but the other part of his mind told him that he liked what was happening to him and that he should keep listening to what Paul was telling him to do. The sun was high when they arrived at the cabin and there had been long spaces where there was no memory of anything. He thought maybe that happened after he had asked Paul for more of his special brandy. "Even though it tasted like shit," he told me, "I wanted more of it. I wanted more brandy. And that makes me sad. Makes me feel such shame, Keskoua. How can you want to be with me?"

I knew Paul Le Putois had put pain medicine in the brandy. Monsieur St-Amand had told Cougar about it and he told me. But I said nothing. Only caressed Falcon's brow and leaned up and over to kiss it.

"Don't," he said. "Let me finish the story. Shame wants me to bury it again—what I did. No. I think 'drown it' is the better expression?" And he smiled that special with-the-eyes-but-not-with-the-mouth smile of his.

This made me happy.

"Keep going," I told him. "Tell me everything. Paul Le Putois was not a bad man, was he?"

"No, he was not. He was not a good man! But he was not a bad man. Nothing like his… his father."

"So tell me more. What kind of things did you see when you were in the cabin at Mouse Ridge? Did you see Jean-Baptiste Bourque and how he died? Was his spirit there? Tell me more. Does this condition of stopping liquor give you visions of the future. Does it work better than the plant we get from our neighbors, the Malecites? Maybe this is a good thing for our young people when they go onto the land to learn what their gift is. What do—"

Falcon's face turned very sad right then and he grabbed hold of my wrist so hard it hurt me.

"Stop it," I said. "You are getting to be like Claude with this grabbing me all the time and looking at me with such eyes on you. What's wrong?"

"I saw things that were not good visions. They were from the White man's liquor. I have experienced the Sweat Lodge many times and what goes on in the Sweat Lodge and what went on with me in the cabin at Mouse Ridge were so far from each other that… that…"

He went quiet again so I told myself to keep my mouth as shut as I could but I'm not very good at that so I asked him: "What were the things you saw that you knew were not there?"

"I heard drumming and voices," he said and his eyes were getting big like Paul Le Putois's eyes. "I saw impossible insects. They were impossible. Huge. Fourteen legs. Twelve legs. No legs, then fifty! Sometimes they were flying around my head. Trying to get into my ears, into my brain. I heard people walking around outside but they never did anything until near the end—near the end when I heard many men shouting and I heard a gunshot and I heard Paul cry out that he'd been struck." Falcon's eyes went to the floor. "I didn't believe that either at first. Not until they let me out and offered me brandy. *This'll get you back on your feet,* was what that big man, Charles, said to me. But I didn't trust him."

"Hmm," I said. "One-Eyed Joe doesn't like him either. I think they know each other from a long time ago."

"He's a wolverine that one."

"With the clenched-jaw illness," I suggested, more to myself. "Tell me more."

"Even with his pain, Paul told me not to take the bottle from Charles. Claude and Mathieu agreed and took the bottle away and Claude poured it on the ground." Falcon looked away from me. "People care a lot more about me than I thought they did."

I caressed his cheek. "Yes, we do, oqoti, dear one."

"Little Cock tried to get me to drink from *his* bottle then, but I think he was happy when I didn't take any. He drank most of it really quick. Afraid Claude would take it and pour it out, too, I guess."

We laughed at that even though it wasn't funny.

"Who shot Paul? Was it Little Cock?"

"I didn't see it happen, but no. I saw lots of things, but not that… I was still seeing things and sometimes I still am."

Almost as though he had been listening outside the door, Monsieur St-Amand entered the room at that moment to say, "He needs to sleep right now, Keskoua. Come with me, Falcon."

☽ ○ ☾

Later in the village, I got the other part of the story from those who had been there when Paul got shot.

Claude said that he and Mathieu had caught up with the group almost right away because somebody had decided to send Little Cock, musket and all, back to get some liquor from the fort. He wasn't a very good hunter because the animals could always smell alcohol off him but he knew the bush and shortcuts like nobody else and he could run like a snipe and that's where he got his name from. They also sent him because they didn't want him involved in the planning of anything, Mathieu said. "Whatever Little Cock suggests always involves violence. We didn't want any of that."

"No. We didn't," said Claude, shaking his head sadly. "That's the last thing we wanted."

"But that's not what happened," I said. "Is it?" I was angry. "Who shot him? Who shot Paul Le Putois?"

"I did," Charles said, proud as a drumming grouse with three or four females watching him instead of a few men and me. "It was I who done it." He raised his musket arm high.

"In the stomach?" I said, horrified. "It's worse than a snake bite when the stomach stuff gets in the blood."

"He did it on purpose," said Claude.

"I finally got the whore's son for killing my friend."

"What friend? Say it," said Claude, his jaw tight.

"Jean-Baptiste Bourque, bien sûr."

"Bourque? Jean-Baptiste Bourque? The man who forced himself on my woman?" One-Eyed Joe came from behind me to my right side. Half blind, he had to squeeze his eyes to see. "I know now for sure who this mi'jan is. This excrement. It's Le Gros. I recognized his stink but did not want to believe it could be him. Could not believe he would dare return."

Claude and Mathieu shuffled closer to Charles and from my other side, Jacques l'Itale and Dancing Raven moved in. Charles was now surrounded. I saw Gi'gwesu run away, fast, in the direction of the fort.

One-Eyed Joe stepped in front of me so I now had to watch from beside his head. "He was there at Mouse Ridge the day Jean-Baptiste Bourque—" he spat on the ground "—hurt Young Rabbit Woman."

The men around Charles grumbled and moved in even closer, some with their hands on the hilts of their knives. This made the spirit of a squirrel run up the back of my neck. I couldn't imagine what might be running up the back of the neck of Charles Le Gros.

"La Grossesse here was lined up to be next."

"Le Putois drew first," said Charles. "And don't call me that or I'll—"

"You'll what?" said One-Eyed Joe and he spat on the ground again.

"Drew first?" said Jacques l'Itale. "With what? A stick of bannock? He had no weapon in his hand. He hadn't seen us coming. He was reaching down for a sack of food."

I could see Little Cock—half a bottle of brandy in one hand, his musket in the other—approaching the group from behind Charles. Claude and Mathieu were not aware of this until he spoke. "Hey. What's going on?"

They turned and Charles took this opportunity to try to bolt but One-Eyed Joe was too fast for him and jutted his foot out to trip him. Charles hit the ground with his face and sat up rubbing dirt out of his mouth. "Tabernacle. What's wrong with you guys? I did everybody a service by getting rid of that démon. Chalice, il était fou. Très fou. Even crazier than you, Little Cock." With some difficulty he got himself up to a standing position again and once again the men barred his escape.

"What the fuck you gon' do now, Le Gros?" asked Little Cock, stupid drunk and laughing.

"You were there, Little Cock," said Claude. "When he shot Le Putois."

"So? What's wrong with that? He's right. Le Putois was crazy."

"No reason to shoot a man," said Jacques l'Itale. "Especially in the stomach. You think that's acceptable?" He leaned away from his position beside Charles to get close to Little Cock's face. "Your daughter's right about you. You're a mean one."

Little Cock stepped back and his bottle hit the ground as he lifted his musket up at Jacques l'Itale's chest. "Want to feel what it's like to get it in the heart? I told you before. Leave my daughter alone."

Claude stepped in and tried to soothe both men. "Enough of this. We have a funeral to prepare for."

Just then, Gi'gwesu came back into view followed by several soldiers, muskets held in both hands, ready to fire at a moment's notice.

One of the soldiers demanded "What's going on here?"

"Exactly what *I* wanted to know," said Little Cock with his musket still pointed at Jacques l'Itale's chest. "I want this foreigner arrested."

A signal from the senior soldier allowed two soldiers to let their muskets swing on their straps to move beside Charles. They grabbed his arms as a third soldier moved behind him.

"Not him, you idiots. This one." And when Little Cock tried to indicate Jacques l'Itale with his musket again, he staggered and nearly fell.

Two more soldiers swung their muskets behind them and a third removed Little Cock's musket from his grasp. They easily lifted him up in the air by his elbows. Kicking and screaming, he tried to get away but it was of no use.

In no time, Charles Le Gros and Little Cock had been taken away by the soldiers to be locked up.

"He shot him in the stomach on purpose?" I asked Claude. "Poor Paul. How long…" Tears were coming now and they made my voice break. "How long…"

"Come with me," he said. "Mathieu and I will tell you everything."

☽ ○ ☾

Charles Le Gros, a man nobody had seen around for many summers had shown up out of nowhere, determined to kill Paul Le Putois. We thought maybe he had been reminded of what Le Putois had done to Jean-Baptiste

Bourque because we were all looking for Paul's mother, Geneviève, and Paul's name went around. We thought Le Gros could have been around for a long time before Paul Le Putois took Falcon away and this was Le Gros's chance to make Paul Le Putois look bad to give Le Gros an excuse to get away with killing him.

Sometimes people get revenge stuck in their heads and they want to get rid of somebody who had killed a relative or friend of theirs, but not very many people wanted to make their death hurt as much as possible. Charles Le Gros didn't shoot Le Putois in the head, he didn't shoot him in the heart. He shot him in the stomach. Nobody did that. Nobody. Even Paul Le Putois wouldn't do that to anybody. Paul Le Putois was a coward—everybody knew enough not to call him that to his face—but if he was going to kill you, he would do it fast. Paul wasn't one to make anybody suffer. At least not on purpose, like I said about him before.

It made me feel sad to remember Paul Le Putois when his eyes were like the eyes of an owl and when he had frightened me and all the other children—and some of the older people, too.

What Paul Le Putois had done was lock Falcon in the coureurs de bois cabin at Mouse Ridge with nothing but food and water and healing potions so he would dry out from the liquor and maybe learn how much trouble it could be if he kept on drinking it.

"Geneviève is the one who killed Father Soucy," said Claude. "Paul told us as he lay dying. He didn't want the blame to be on anybody else. Especially on his mother but he knew she didn't have any choice. She didn't want to kill Father Soucy. He was trying to kill her and Paul was there as a witness."

And I knew why. The Father was not about to tell all of us that he had been lying, that he wasn't a real Father so he got her up on top of The Bear by getting two of our little ones to go and tell her that I was up there having my baby and needed her help.

But he had got up there himself and had hung a rope down for her and was hiding and calling out with a high voice like a woman's. "Help me. Help me."

Geneviève, with great difficulty because of the way she was bent, got up on top of The Bear but there was no Keskoua and this worried her very much. She went to the edge to see if I had fallen off and that was when the Father came out from behind a stunted bush and tried to push her over. She fought with everything she had against him, screaming and yelling for help, kicking and biting and pulling his hair. She had vowed never ever to be abused by a man again and she was being true to her word.

Kji Niskam was kind to her that day because it just so happened that Paul Le Putois was going by behind The Bear like he preferred to do but it wasn't his usual day. He told the men that he'd had a feeling and that's why he went that day.

While he was dying, he asked One-Eyed Joe if this meant he might have been forgiven by God for all the bad things he had done in his life and would be able to go on the special Journey that our people took when they died. One-Eyed Joe told him yes and so did Falcon and a couple of the others. That made me feel good that Paul Le Putois was at least happy about dying even though it was hurting so bad he could hardly talk at all. But he did.

He got up on The Bear and saw that the Father was trying to push his mother off its back. I think Paul Le Putois had made a promise to himself, like his mother had, to never let anybody hurt a woman again because he went right away to help her get away from the Father. He saw that the Father was hanging over the edge of the rock and holding onto his mother's dress and his mother was holding onto a tree there. The dress was ripping but the Father was still pulling her down along with him.

Paul said he didn't want her to fall and he didn't want the Father to fall either. He still believed that the Father was a Father and knew enough of our ways to know that if she killed a Father she would be cursed and so would her son and any children that her son might have, and grandchildren, too. Paul Le Putois had never before taken an interest in any woman—except for me, but I think he loved me more like a sister, like Claude loved me—but he thought at that point, he would like to have children. Maybe he could be a better father than his own had been.

"He crawled up her dress," Le Putois told Claude and the others "and then he was up on the back of The Bear again and once more trying to push her off but—and I never saw my mother act like that—she grabbed his hair and she brought his head down at the same time she brought her knee up into it. I heard the crack of his nose when it broke. He grabbed her dress again and the torn piece came off and it floated down the rock like a bat that forgot where the hole to its cave was. It floated then slipped sideways then came to rest.

"'Then he went over. I don't know how, but then he went over and I was there beside the edge and I saw him hit the rocks as he went down and down and down and I saw his brains coming out and flying all over the place but..."

And Claude said this part made him cry and he could see the other men turn their faces away from each other, too, because those who knew Paul Le Putois and what he had to go through when he was a little one, knew that all that pain came out of him right then when he said the next thing he said:

"But it didn't scare me. I knew from then I would never be afraid of anything again in my life. And that's when I knew that I had to do something good for somebody. That's when I decided..." He moaned, Claude told me, a mournful sound that came from his toes even though he was smiling and his eyes had stopped being big and round.

"He smiled," said Claude, and Mathieu rubbed a rough knuckle under an eye and nodded. "He smiled and said 'That's when I decided I had to help Falcon. He's a good man. He would make a good man for Keskoua and I love her. But I didn't think Kji Niskam would need to exchange my life for his. But it's good. It's good… I'm going on a special Journey.' And then he died."

Twenty-six

Nobody saw Geneviève around the village any more—at least to talk to her to see if she was real or not. People would see a flash of dress behind a tree or over by The Bear the same as her son, Paul Le Putois, used to make us see all the time. But we didn't know for sure. Because of what Paul Le Putois had done to help Falcon and Young Rabbit Woman—and even his own mother when he was little—we believed his spirit was sacred now. Not for killing anybody, but for trying to save somebody else from getting killed or dying. From the time we wake up from our dreams in the morning until the time we go back to dreaming when the sun goes to sleep behind the hills, we decide what to do many, many times. The first decision we do every day is a simple one: shall I light a fire or relieve myself first? The next decision could be: shall I eat or have something to drink first? As the day goes by, more and more decisions step in front of us, wanting us to choose them and some of those choices can make us hated if we choose the wrong one and they can make us hated even if we choose to do what's right. We all had great respect for Paul Le Putois and what he had sacrificed to help Falcon and by doing that, help me, too.

But because some people refused to believe that the Father had not been a Father, they said God had killed Geneviève somehow and now her spirit was cursed to roam the land forever in sadness and she would never be able to go on the Journey to the land of our ancestors. Others said she was not dead but only afraid of everybody now and not just pure White people but those of our people who were mixed. There were more and more of us mixed now so to me that would make sense if she was afraid of us all—she wouldn't know who she could trust anymore because we were all starting to look the same. She had always trusted me, so I was hurt that she didn't come to talk to me if she was having problems with her fears again. But if she was truly dead, then I guess she couldn't. I only hoped, no matter which one it might be, that she would finally get some kind of peace by wandering the land.

Charles Le Gros went to trial and was executed by firing squad only two moons after he had shot Paul Le Putois in the stomach.

Feather and her soldier got together finally and had a baby boy. Falcon and I got married. Sleeping Cougar took Falcon's sister, Gentle Robin Wing as his wife, but even before that she had started talking to me and being nice to me.

Marguerite got her "shipment" of sheep from The Colonies delivered one night after dark and started up a small business making and selling products from their wool and skins. True to her word, she taught me how to spin wool and weave on a loom.

I would like to be able to tell you that life in our village was smooth and that everybody was happy but there was a lot of trouble with the English now—the people Marguerite always liked to call "les maudits anglaises." I was starting to understand why she called them that. They were different from the French who had come to live among us here in l'Acadie. I also heard more and more often that the French who had come here were different from the French at the settlement at Québec, too. The French who had come here—even the craziest of the coureurs de bois—

respected our ways along with their own and this made things even better for all of us because we used their ways to make our lives better, too. We lived with each other and took husbands and wives from each other so were slowly becoming not each other anymore but something different and beautiful. The English didn't like that. Some of them would take their handkerchiefs from their pockets whenever we were around and put them to their noses and turn away like we were some dead animal they found on the trail, one that had been there for a couple of nights and days. We never knew when there might be a raid at the fort with guns going off and scaring away the animals that we needed for food. Even Orignal-Sale's grandchildren's children were frightened by the noises and wanted to run away into the bush. We all decided to leave the fighting to the soldiers and tried to just stay away from there more and more.

E'e, things were different now. I often awoke with the crying eyes of The Bear staring into mine. At first I thought it was my imagination that it kept looking sadder and sadder because I didn't think it could look any sadder than it had the first time I saw it. But I was wrong. The English took over the land and the French soldiers went back to their King and that was the end of each other.

Glossary of Mi'gmaw Terms

apalqaqamej: chipmunk
app: repeat [please]; what did you say?
atu'tuej: squirrel
e'e: yes
elue'wiet: crazy
emtesgit: arrogant, snooty
gesgamugwa'latl, gesgamugwa'toq: make vanish, make disappear, dissolve
gesmi'sit: speak in odd or unusual way; speak with a heavy accent
gesm'pisit: strange clothes
gi'gwesu: muskrat
Haudenosaunee: a Nation ("Iroquois")
kaksk'us, kaksk'ug: cedar(s)
Lnu Saqamaw: Chief
lutmaqan: gossip, rumor, hearsay
mesgei': I am sorry
Mi'gmaw, Mi'gmaq: Eastern Nation of Aboriginal People
mi'jan: excrement
moqopa'q: wine
natawinpiteget: good healer
na to'q: all right, OK
snawe'l, snawe'g: sugar tree(s), maple(s)
Wendat: a Nation ("Huron")

References

Most of the Mi'gmaw terms came from:

http://www.mikmaqonline.org/

Most of the research about the Guidry family came from:

http://www.ancestry.com/

About the Author

On her paternal grandmother's side, Sherrill Wark is a descendant of "the Frenchman Claude Guidry" and Marguerite Petitpas through their son Pierre Guidry dit LaBine.

www.ingramcontent.com/pod-product-compliance
Ingram Content Group UK Ltd.
Pitfield, Milton Keynes, MK11 3LW, UK
UKHW020143250726
13967UKWH00002B/830